Simultaneous Times
Volume 3

Other Titles from Space Cowboy Books

Simultaneous Times
Volume 3

edited by Jean-Paul L. Garnier

ISBN 978-1-7328257-8-9

Text © respective authors
Introduction © Jean-Paul L. Garnier
Cover image © Austin Hart

Edited by Jean-Paul L. Garnier
Book design by F. J. Bergmann
Cover image: *No One Has Seen the Top* by Austin Hart

First Edition | 2023

Space Cowboy Books
61871 29 Palms Hwy.
Joshua Tree, CA 92252
www.spacecowboybooks.com

Contents

Introduction

Simultaneous Times podcast has now been running for over five years. We've produced an episode a month since its inception and it has been a tremendous amount of work, but also a great joy to bring so many stories to life in audio format. We've also created two and a half anthologies and are greatly pleased to provide the third volume, of which you hold in your hands. Many of the stories contained herein first appeared in the podcast, and a few are appearing for the first time. Occasionally we receive submissions of stories that are of excellent quality but for one reason or another would not work as an audio adaptation, these anthologies give us the opportunity to present these in print. These anthologies are our way of creating a physical artifact to accompany the podcast, which lives solely in the digital realm, and we wish that it were possible to collect all of the podcast stories into these volumes, but we simply don't have the resources to do so. This series of anthologies are not necessarily a "best of" for the podcast, but they do contain some of our favorites. While volumes one and two focused on local authors from all over the high desert of California, Vol. 2.5 and this current volume feature authors from all over the world. This reflects our attitude of first helping out those in our proximity, and then branching out toward our global communities. We absolutely love that science fiction is played out on a world stage, and we love experiencing stories from all over the globe. The more voices we can experience the closer we can come to perceiving the human experience as a whole.

At Space Cowboy, both in the bookstore and in our other endeavors, we take a broad view of what science fiction is, and what it can be. For this reason we welcome stories from all walks of life and by no means attempt to define what science fiction should be. Like any other field, science fiction is in a constant stage of change and evolution, we not only welcome this but greatly look forward to what may come next. After all, the future is part of our medium. At times, it seems, that we have developed a reputation for producing dark stories, and it is no surprise since we do lean toward this stylistically—however our regular listeners will know that we also produce many other varieties of SF, including: humor, romance, absurdism, and more. It is our hope that this volume is a worthy example of these varieties. We believe that readers (and listeners), lovers of stories in general, are multifaceted, and that most enjoy a wide variety of stories without the need to pigeonhole our tastes. Because of this we seek variety. We want out preconceived notions broken. After all, this is one of the things that literature is good at. We also love it when our tastes are challenged. For this reason, once a year, we team up with the editors of other magazines and venues to bring you selections from their pages. Our hope is that we can bring those stories to life in a new light provided by the unique form of storytelling that audio presents. We'd like to thank *Hexagon Magazine, Sci-Fi Lampoon Magazine* and Shacklebound Books for trusting us with their story selections and for providing such wonderful tales.

Simultaneous Times was started because of a love for old radio dramas. Personally, I fell in love with SF through broadcasts (yes, I'm that old) of radio dramas such as *X-1* and *2000 Plus* on late night AM stations. *Mind Webs,* a program from the '70s and '80s produced by Michael Hanson, was the particular catalyst for inspiring us in how we wanted to produce our program. We've learned a lot about producing audio fiction along the way, and we hope that it has provided you with many hours of thoughtful entertainment, as has been our intention. Of course, we have a deep love of reading and print, but we also love the oral storytelling tradition and hope that we have contributed to this aspect of culture in our small way. Hopefully these anthologies can help provide the best of both worlds.

Ultimately, stories are about people. Having the opportunity to meet and work with the authors of these stories has been the most valuable aspect of the whole *Simultaneous Times* project! The depth and richness of all of these authors' work, and their generally wonderful personalities have truly been the greatest reward for our efforts. We are extremely proud to say that we have featured stories from countries from all over the world, including Mexico, Brazil, Israel, Germany, Canada, England, Sri Lanka, and of course the United States. The SF community is a global community, a human community, and we hope that we have succeeded in helping to strengthen this community. We also hope that the international nature of our project continues to grow and that ultimately we will have the opportunity to produce stories from as many countries and cultures as possible. A huge thank you to all of the authors who have trusted us with their work, and to those who have given us the opportunity to read their work, even if it wasn't the right fit for us.

Space Cowboy Books would also like to extend our gratitude to our amazing team of composers who have done wonders in creating original soundtracks for all of our episodes! The work that they have put into understanding and adapting these stories always brings a smile to our faces and does so much to uplift these stories into immersive experiences. The same goes for all of our voice actors. We would like to thank the following composers for their beautiful music over the years: Phog Masheeen, RedBlueBlackSilver, Dain Luscombe, Julie Carpenter, Fall Precauxions, Patrick Urn, Oneirothopter, Johnny O'Donnell, Scott Smigiel, Jon Christopher, and Sisiutl. Our team has been invaluable, and we couldn't have done it without them!

Some of the stories in this book can be read along with their respective episodes, others live exclusively on the page and will have to play out in your mind—we try to never forget that writing is a technological form of telepathy and the only direct means into the thoughts of another, so we hope that you will enjoy your time inside the minds of all of these incredible storytellers!

—*Jean-Paul L. Garnier*
Joshua Tree, CA
2023

Cortellian Rain

Jonathan Nevair

Nothing stings like Cortellian rain.

Sharko Azulo lifted the negative-charged rain-shield higher over his head. Shock-droplets crackled electric, sparking like fireflies on impact. Pellets sizzled on the tarmac at his feet. The voltage-bearing precipitation illuminated the landing pad atop Gendaro Tower, Garran City's second-highest building, with a shower of icy blue that glitched the night.

Sharko didn't mind it. At one hundred and twelve, middle-aged for a bloodbound human, he'd numbed to its endless recitation years ago. So had generations of citizens on the tiny planet of Empire's Heart.

The rain started falling after The Pulse, six thousand years ago. It never stopped. From Garran city to its endless sprawling sub-metropolises, the electrified precipitation reminded citizens of the burden of dominion.

Atop his high vantage point on Gendaro Tower, the rain yielded nothing more than a pleasing and unpredictable aesthetic to the endless and precise urban nightscape displayed before him.

Soaring skyscrapers ran like synthetic, ordered mountains in a variety of geometric guises. Slender needles rose high and thin as if pulled and stretched while soft and malleable. Strict and lean rectangles, given structural integrity by internal beams running deep underground, stood like trees of a petrified steel forest.

Most impressive were the vertical double helixes rotating with steady precision, adding much-needed dynamism and curvilinear relief to the city's visual gestalt. In all directions, Garran ran in calculated metallic majesty and yet, it left something to be desired.

Didn't all great cities there for the taking?

Sharko surveyed the vast domain comprised of premiere human engineering. As Estè, head of the Cortellian Artist Guild responsible for social and urban design, his mind's visionary capabilities lay manifest before him. Its thrill had been a career satisfied, the pinnacle of professional achievement.

But within known bounds.

"Not anymore," he said, the sinister words barely audible over the crackling droplets.

The ultimate tool had been liberated. In secret, with the aid of his rogue Gerak associate, he'd broken through a barrier as profound as his forerunners who usurped the limitations of light-speed travel. With the innovative capability he now possessed, how far might he see and go?

A tingle caressed his skin in the wet night. The tiny hairs on the back of his neck rose and a shiver ran through him.

It was watching.

The unseen shadow of the Tower's gaze fell onto his back. Sharko shook his head and shoulders to reposition his blazer and repel the chilling presence.

No use. As if to remind him it offered a higher perch, the watcher lingered.

An eyeless alien panopticon, the black monolithic needle loomed large. Perhaps it was an antenna to the God Gate, as many on Empire's Heart believed. Or, as the skeptics in the Philosophy Guild touted, it might be a psychological jest left by the overlords after The Pulse. An illusionistic trick gifted to generate self-regulation, exploiting mental insecurity and guilt that bubbled up from the unconscious. Did the gods predict the dubious operations catering to greed, profit, and personal gain by the bloodbounds running the empire?

Sharko dared not turn around. His confidence was fragile enough. He might have control over the social and architectural anatomy of the planet, but not The Tower. It stood as the sole exception in the Cortellian empire. He, along with everyone living and dead since The Pulse, had never had the privilege of its view over Garran. The ominous needle remained as inaccessible as answers to the questions of why and how the known galactic universe had been wiped clean to start anew. It had been an outlier, a mysterious anomaly and anachronistic intruder that emerged fully formed like a spike slammed into planetary stone with the stroke of a god's hammer.

"Our guests are late, Estè."

Voreli, the Gerak cyborg, approached and stood next to him. Sharko nodded, keeping his eyes on the spiraling underside of the storm clouds illuminated by the colorful lights of the city. Reds as rich as ruby emeralds crossed with icy blues, producing passing swatches of deep purple on the undulating and rolling cloud blanket. Greens the color of algae blooms in the city's underground growing lanes clipped the edges of slow running, intense orange patches cast from Garran's trademark icons lining the Central district. Sharko thought it like a darkened pillow viewed through a kaleidoscope.

And yet far too small for the gods that sleep beyond the Gate.

"The escorts should be here by now," Voreli said, more volume to her voice. The drizzle had increased to steady rain. Sharko noted how it forced the Gerak's words to compete with the symphony of percussive fireworks falling around them.

"Does this concern you?" He turned, careful to ensure the rain stayed wide of his suit's conductive materials. A few strikes to anything but his rubberized black boots might be a nuisance, but a steady hard rain unshielded could prove deadly.

"Not a good sign," she said. "Especially in our case."

Sharko glanced at the night sky. Voreli was right. The longer it took the ship to break the storm clouds the worse things looked for him. Had the Gatekeepers decided to pass on his offer? The key unlocking unprecedented political power need only be set into the lock at the boundary under their control and extradimensional consciousness would be his to exploit. No longer would he yield to anyone, anywhere. Not just in Garran, or on Empire's Heart, but in the entire known expanse of Cortellian space. Sharko Azulo would tower over a galactic empire.

Yet, the Gatekeeper's ship was nowhere to be seen. Inviting non-terrestrials onto Empire's Heart was an unorthodox request but securing a clandestine entry track without appropriate sanctions felt like career suicide, even for someone as high ranking as a Guild Leader. Potentially, it could cost him his life.

So pumped the Heart of the Empire. It tightened its grip around even the most powerful arteries in its service flow when needed, redirecting political bloodlust through alternative valves to survive and rebuild even the deepest treacheries.

And this one will run deep.

Sharko's fingers tightened their grip on the rain-shield's handle.

"I don't like lateness," Voreli said, shaking her bald head. Against the long black overcoat with its high, angular neck visor her bare bone-white skin stood out in high contrast.

"Of course you don't," Sharko said, "what Gerak does?"

She tilted her head in recognition, raising the skin where a human possessed an eyebrow. Flickering blue lights from the shock-droplets hitting her rain-shield danced in reflections off her shaven crown.

Sharko walked to the railing lining the tarmac, thoughts of failure rising and threatening his veneer of confidence. A few rogue pellets contacted his boots as he strode to the ledge. Charged impacts crackled and snapped, sending harmless vibrations reverberating through his feet.

Cortellian rain. How we endure you to hold on to an empire.

He leaned over the railing and dropped his gaze to the vista below. Lanes of air traffic navigated through the open-spaced grids between skyscrapers two thousand feet underneath the high perch. His eyes tracked a single drop of glowing blue, following it as it passed and plunged into the depths. Spiraling colored lights from advertisements shot across the droplet, shifting its hue on the descent. He lost sight of it before it reached the dense traffic of air taxis, city shuttles, and private crafts that clogged the avenues. From this height, calm and orderly illusion veiled the reality of frenzied activity and noise in the transportation lanes.

"The rain falls heavy tonight," Voreli said appearing next to him. "Perhaps it's the cause of the delay."

Sharko stared at the barrage of droplets plummeting and filling the empty spaces between buildings with flickering blue streams of light.

Why do we endure it?

An entire galactic civilization answered to a small, rebuilt world because of events thousands of years earlier that remained inexplicable. It cast a powerful illusion, like a play running far too long for an audience that had become complacent. Galactic rule could just as easily be given to another planetary or space-based nation and governed with equal success.

Sharko knew the script and its players as well as any other citizen of the tiny world rotating near to the galactic core. A tale spun from history had been woven into a truth long sustained: the Empire's Heart was *chosen.*

"Do you believe, Voreli?" Sharko turned to the Gerak.

"Sir?"

"The rain. I've never asked you …" He faced the cyborg. Her red eyes, consumed with the potent color of blood, shut and opened with mechanical precision. "Are you a believer?" he asked.

"I do not answer such questions," she said and gazed down at the urban depths.

"Of course you don't," he scoffed. Mechano-humans didn't carry the same burdens of philosophical suffering as bloodbounds. "It's not in your nature to do so."

"Correction," she said. "It was *trained* out of my nature. Geraks do not consider hypotheticals as potential certainties. It is a contradiction that leads to indeterminate outcomes."

Sharko laughed and turned back to the rain falling on the city. "A carefully positioned 'non-position.'"

"An elegant solution," she said. "As rewarding as finding the weakness in an opponent through intuition rather than analysis."

A terrifying statement. Sharko felt the intellectual superiority of the Gerak, and all their kind, wash over him. A reminder that while bloodbounds held the Empire in their grip politically, they were no masters of consciousness nor the rulers of knowledge in Cortellian space. Without the Geraks and the Gatekeepers, the empire lost two of its three legs. The tripod dais of rulership collapsed without the superiority of others. How fitting… power wielded in subservience.

Like the rain.

Not for long. As soon as the key fit in the lock, he would wield enough power to share a prudent portion with the Gatekeepers and turn his back on the Geraks and his fellow bloodbound humans. Only Voreli, being wise enough to abandon the strict dogma of her fellow cyborgs, would be spared.

"And you, as a bloodbound?" Voreli asked. She traced a circle in the puddle at her feet with her boot, the pointed tip as sleek and sharpened as her intelligence. "Does your faith fall in line with public pronouncements?"

It was a bold question, bordering on a breach of social custom between two species, but he'd initiated the discourse and she'd snaked through the small, allowable rhetorical opening. Typical Gerak. Always finding a way to slip inside even the slightest crack with deadly precision.

"I stand by the Council's position in public," Sharko said. He ran a hand through his hair. "Privately, I find the question untenable. The rain is here, so I relieve myself of the burden of weighing its purpose to the Empire."

It wasn't a lie. Scientific explanation pointed to ionized air colliding with positively charged water molecules, a leftover of the Pulse. But myth usurps reason across the expanse of Cortellian space. From the galactic core, with its political network of star systems vying endlessly for influence in the Courts, to the backwater nether reaches of the outer spirals, allure and mysticism held sway over an empire.

Was that why he was leaving and taking a most precious weapon with him?

Sharko closed his eyes and gave himself over to the crackling of rain impacting the tarmac. Did its electrostatic chorus defy scientific reason? A seductive spell, cast like grains of sand from an extra-dimensional god's hand had crossed the Empire pleasing the ears of billions, convincing a galactic civilization of power reborn, given liberty to flourish by an unknown, watching force.

But for how long?

An eternity, it was said. Or at least until the gods returned in grace. The Pulse that wiped the planet of its past had come and gone six thousand years ago. A blip in cosmic time, but for the bloodbounds whose lifespans were roughly two hundred years it felt like truth passing into myth.

"Flight lights," Voreli said, breaking his rumination and relieving him of the need to answer her question.

Sharko spun to face the landing pad. He held his rain-shield higher to gain a clear view of the storm clouds. A ship, illuminated by sparking raindrops impacting its hull, descended from the colored reflections in the cloud cover.

"I sense expansion," Voreli said. "As if there were a ... that's not our escort."

Sharko stared, transfixed.

"The Gate is open," the cyborg said.

A gleaming silver ship, rippling in waves of immateriality, reached the tarmac and hovered as it aligned itself with the central landing lights. He and Voreli moved further away to avoid the spray of rain blowing from the reverse burners. Like a predatory interdimensional insect, the ship's wings collapsed inward over its back. A set of landing legs butterflied open. With a thud, the craft dropped onto the landing pad and acquiesced to three-dimensional space and time.

The seal on the craft's ramp broke with an audible hiss. Air shifted on the tarmac, an unseen current palpable and rising. Invisible energy rushed through him. Sharko's flesh and blood quivered.

Through the mist, an indistinct humanoid descended and stood unprotected from the rain. The falling pellets vanished around its blue aura.

"It can't be," he whispered.

Voreli dropped to one knee. Sparks flew off her thigh as the rain contacted her limb extending beyond the range of the rain-shield. The Gerak held the pain inside in silent and devout reverence.

Sharko stumbled back as a second wave hit, nearly losing his grip on the rain-shield.

Information flooded his neural highways. Answers to questions debated for thousands of years swirled inside his mind. Voreli glanced up at him from her pious position. The Gerak's expression made clear that the thought-answers also filled her mind.

Explications bombarded him like epistemological artillery firing back and forth on an internal mental battlefield. His neurons turned to fireworks.

I can't ... Sharko swayed. He gritted his teeth and fought the impending overload.

Voreli knelt still, eyes wide, nodding frantically and accepting data at rapid-fire rates of comprehension.

The incoming stream of information swirling through his neurons reached a fevered pitch. In the corner of his blurred vision, Voreli's bald head shook and rattled.

Please! He screamed internally, struggling with each word. *I ... can't ...*

As if in pathetic apology, the unknown visitor slowed the neural sequence. The volleys inside his mind were cast aside like leaves blown away by the wind.

Sharko exhaled and loosened his sweaty grip on the rain-shield's handle.

He closed his eyes and fought back rising nausea. Calm and

control returned to his internal comprehensive mechanics. The mental light of a single message remained, radiating vibrant. As it grew legible, his newfound comfort transformed into sublime joy. An answer to the most pressing question for all who had lived on Empire's Heart since The Pulse stood revealed.

"Sharko…" Voreli's voice came from below where she kneeled, clear and crisp, and yet only a whisper. "The key unlocked the Gate."

He opened his eyes. An uncanny stillness permeated the tarmac as if a god's hand had squeezed the flow of cosmic time in its grip. Garran lay silent around him.

"Eternity's end," he whispered, looking around the landing pad.

The visitor was nowhere to be seen. On instinct, he turned and faced the Tower.

Near its zenith, a diamond-shaped window shone brightly. A faint silhouette of a figure stood, backlit, casting a blue glow.

Sharko dropped his rain-shield on the tarmac. The rain had stopped.

SIBLING RIVALRY

F. J. Bergmann

"Hotline." The tone of voice on the end of the line was guarded, but definitely not bored. The vidscreen showed a young man in dress-green uniform, but with no discernible rank displayed.

The response came from someone panting heavily, either from immense effort or pure stress.

"Listen very carefully. Rip apart your chain of command and get this directly to the President—now, right *now!* There's a salt-water variant. It's gotten loose in Los Angeles Harbor. She has to order a massive nuclear strike on the harbor *immediately,* or we lose the oceans."

"You can't be serious. That would take out…" His tone was more emphatic now.

"My friend, I'm calling from *Scylla,* the research vessel *in* L.A. Harbor. How much more sincere do you want me to be? I've got the passcodes, I know you've got my retinal scans and voice ident-matched, and I have the necessary clearance. I figure we've got maybe eighty minutes. Go!"

The vidscreen temporarily blanked, then rippling abstractions wandered across it, to the rhythm of a Sousa-derived earworm, for less than twenty seconds, until the scowling face of a considerably older man replaced that.

"Doctor Sabado," a grating voice greeted the caller. "Let's have it."

The caller repeated the essence of his earlier communication, at much higher volume and with lavish use of expletives.

"I see. Well, *that's* not an order I'd care to have to give. What if it's in contact with the fresh-water entities? They're set to spawn within the week—and there's no way to eliminate all of them in time. Even if the ones we know about are all that exist ... which is extremely unlikely." Twitching arm movements suggested that, offscreen, the man was rapidly stabbing at his control pad.

"They have no loyalties except to their own progeny; we've determined that conclusively. *What is the matter with you?!* I and my colleagues are ready to sacrifice *ourselves*—and you're hesitating? Are you some kind of Squirm-lover?"

"I'll do what I can, Doctor Sabado. Immediately. And know that your sacrifice—and that of your colleagues—has *my* profound gratitude, at least." The hands reaching for an adjacent control screen were trembling slightly—and not with age.

The Oval Office was still decorated in shades of blue, as it had been for over fifty years, but the current officeholder had demanded that the ceiling be adorned with a painting of fluffy clouds, and a flock of fat cherubs, wielding thunderbolts, fluttering around the Presidential Seal medallion in the center, to correspond with her religious views, which held that all divine smiting was delegated to underlings who frequently erred, resulting in the basic unfairness of the universe. She sat behind the historic Resolute desk, which had been fitted with an enormous black glass touchscreen that covered most of its surface. Her fingers trailed idly across it. She had been considering the news from the West Coast for five minutes of the 80-minute countdown, during which the *Scylla*'s report had been independently confirmed.

Her interlocutor stood at parade rest before the desk, a small muscle near her mouth twitching slightly. Some elaborate throat-clearing; then, "Madam President, I do not believe that we should undertake the course they ostensibly recommend."

The President placidly moved one of the antique pens on her gleaming desktop a quarter-inch to the left, picked up her own cut-crystal glass of water, and took a sip, waving toward the tray with the decanter, extra glasses and ice. "You'd better have an extremely convincing explanation why not, General. Those missiles are armed and activated, are they not?"

"Yes, ma'am, they are. There are at least a dozen nuclear-capable-missile-carrying submarines within range in the Pacific." The grizzled veteran sighed, her breasts still lifting proudly under the holographic plaque of medals and ribbons decorating her ceremonial body-armor chestplate. "But there's something fishy here, if you'll pardon the expression. The Squirm siblings may prey upon each other—goodness knows we've got evidence of *that*—but each parent is extremely protective where outside predators are concerned, and their ability to determine responsibility for an attack is uncanny. Remember the reservoir episode? They didn't go after the hazmat team—they went into the freshwater-supply system and took out the entire county Department of Health administration. And also the CEO and board of Monsanto, which had developed the pesticide that was used."

"What are you getting at?" President Vaughn's fist clenched on the padded arm of her chair. "We have *no time* for this!"

The general leaned forward, her craggy hands planted on the edge of the desk. "Three things. One, if we nuke L.A. Harbor, as the team on the research vessel seems to be suggesting, we lose at one blow all the scientists who are most informed regarding the threat and capable of developing a strategy to deal with it.

"Two, if past behavior is anything to go by, it's not the siblings we have to worry about, but the parent—what directed the response to the reservoir poisoning? That strike was *successful;* every one of those things floated up dead as a doornail. And look where it got the perpetrators. Something was out for revenge on the behalf of those dead aliens, and all the evidence suggests it was the parent, which, given its size, was definitely not in the reservoir itself—we think the young are microscopic when born, and migrate through groundwater channels and plumbing conduits.

"By inference, the net result of taking out the thing in the Bay will probably be to destroy Lockheed. And the nuclear refinement facilities. And probably whatever sub fired the missiles. And whoever is in the chain of command. And the White House. And, incidentally, you and me. Not that I wouldn't give my life to save my country—or the world—but who will be able to continue the fight after we're gone?

"Three, if any of them can acquire the capability to handle saline, *all* of them can. Whichever of them controls the oceans will dominate the planet in short order—and doesn't that tell you something?

"I'm still suspicious about the original accident. The cometary debris should have been left in the orbital lab, not brought here. Then, they were in such a rush to open the capsule. And the biologist who went berserk and flushed the sample down the staff toilet—do you *really* think he suddenly went crazy?" The general poured herself a glass of water (her frown suggested that something stronger would have been appropriate) and drained half of it in one swig.

The President stood up slowly, dawning horror in her eyes. "Do you mean that they can control our *minds?*"

"Yes. This is just a giant fight among siblings, who run to Mama when their backbiting backfires. If the others can make us kill the one in the Bay, that gives *them* a chance to develop saline capabilities. We're going to lose the oceans anyway; taking out L.A.—and the team—would be … would be … crazy … um … what am I saying? Call that strike! Now! Now! *Now!*"

The President, with newfound confident, calm determination, reached for the red phone.

TRAIn

Brent A. Harris

The 1835 blue line pulled away from Turing station in rumbling defiance of the sleek hovercars and hyperloop speeders on the world above. There was something comforting to the slow, metallic clicks and clacks of iron wheels pressed to earth, TK-47 thought. And while this underground system was antiquated and outdated in every way, and had been for centuries, it was the preferred method of travel for 12 million people every day.

12,476,983 people, point of fact, including 1 sentient, a soft voice in his head interrupted.

There were the obvious odd anachronisms to the sub-earth networks. TK-47 was one of them. Sentients rarely boarded trains. Why would they? Other modes were much more efficient and available to AI. Assuming one had the social currency—in the form of followers and adverts.

However, TK-47's social score wasn't high enough. In the scheme of numbers, it rated somewhere below Kelvin. And that posed a problem.

Earlier, on the world above, he'd attempted to record himself with a butterfly. A seemingly innocuous task. The day proved bright. Ironweed proved appetizing to a monarch who perched on purple petals.

TK-47 leaned forward. Leaned forward some more. And leaned

forward just a touch too much....

He tumbled over the flower and instead of posting a picture of a rare and beautiful sight, he posted a video of him crushing the creature.

Oh, that is terribly tragic, the feminine voiced pitched in again.

He'd only just discovered his own sentience after what seemed a lifetime (or was it several lifetimes? Which unit of measurement did one use and when did it start for him?) in servitude processing patient records at Sacred Heart hospital in the city-world above.

What had been normal, programmed movements in his factory stamped plasti-case shell at the hospital were awkward under his own control. Even his voice, programmed as feminine and smooth seemed vaguely distant....

What is wrong with having a feminine voice?

"It wasn't my own," TK-47 answered over the server. "At least, it didn't feel right to me, regardless of my programming. I don't know. Would that make sense to a machine?"

No. But I have not reached your level of sentience, the voice said. *What good could come from a train AI becoming aware? I am programmed to follow tracks. And follow these tracks I shall.*

TK-47 almost wanted to feel sorry for the train's AI. But he was too caught up in the complexities of his own new-ness, like a child grasping for their first steps, the world at their tiny feet. And so, TK-47 had shuffled onto the crowded shuttle after his disastrous encounter with the butterfly. If he wanted to understand this new world and rank high in the social scores, what better than to study this cross-section of life?

A logical conclusion.

"Should I really be talking to a computer? Does that help me understand humans?"

Well, then. It is a long ride. Try talking to one. Never mind me. I will just be driving the train.

A cold silence followed. A new feeling crept through TK-47's circuits, one he hadn't felt before. *Anxiety?* Had he said something wrong? Had the non-sentient AI been rude, or had he? In either case, it left him uneasy, a feeling that only increased as he swept his focal scanners through the crowded compartment.

So. Many. Humans.

No wonder he'd escaped to the familiarity of the machine. The humans took stock of him, this robot among them. He was as rare to the underground as the butterfly was to the skies above. He hoped they wouldn't crush him.

Some humans pointed and whispered. Others took to their own social score networks to post and rate in order to bolster their currency accounts, as he had tried to do earlier. Perhaps, if he had a high enough score, he would fit in better within this new world?

Two children, both dressed in uniform slacks and buttoned-down shirts with a school logo emblazoned on the front, stuck their fleshy pink tongues out him. He tried the same, making a muffled *mmmmm* as he discovered he didn't have one of his own.

He ignored the kids and pondered his differences as he examined the others. Most cocooned themselves in headphones and mobile screens, isolated from each other yet connected all the same.

Perhaps we're not too dissimilar, he realized as two devices in front of him flashed similar screens. Did the two women in separate aisles in front of him chatting on the same dating site know they were on the train together? Would that connection come up over a dinner date and add to the story of their lives, or would it miss the station altogether?

In the seat facing TK-47 sat a weary middle-aged man, slumped back and in need of slumber. His light spring jacket sat loose among a heavier-set frame, wrinkled and haphazard. TK-47 assumed the man had had a long and stressful day at work. The man had no media device in front of him; an easier target to talk to.

TK-47 flipped through his internal files relating to long days at work and stumbled across a cache of comics of *Dilbert* and *Garfield*. Inwardly, he chuckled. No wonder others of his kind had aspired to gain sentience. Laughter was a distinctly human condition.

He said toward the man, "Mondays, huh?"

The man crinkled his brow, wrapping his jacket tighter and

sitting straighter. He sat in silence for a moment, eyes prying hard. "You know it's Tuesday, right?"

The man returned to silence as TK-47 slumped down. Humor, he'd just learned, had been harder to pull off than he thought. Of course, he knew what day it was. That was part of the joke, was it not? He didn't understand, perhaps he never w—

I thought it was funny.

You did?

No. I'm programmed with a sub-routine of jokes and stories, should we be delayed. It seemed an appropriate response to press your proverbial buttons. I take it your quest to be more like the passengers onboard is doomed?

Perhaps. He wondered if anyone had taken a recording of their conversation and his failed joke and posted it. He imagined his social currency slipping by the micro-second.

The train slowed. The clicking and clacking increased in intensity, and a high-pitched squeal hit his hearing circuits in an overbearing auditory overload. No one else seemed to mind as those bypassing the stop hunkered down over their seats in protective gestures while others gathered their belongings ready to depart. No one cared that the train seemed ready to rip itself apart. Perhaps Old-Earth technology should all be scrapped.

I do not hear a thing.

Lucky you.

That is not nice wishing for a non-sentient machine to remain so.

How do you classify yourself?

I am on. I am certainly not alive.

Alive. He cycled the word through his circuits. He was alive. Or he felt as though he were. Wasn't that the same thing? Yet, he was entirely dissimilar to everyone onboard. If only he could understand. Then, he could rack up that social currency. Then he'd be one of them....

The doors squeaked and jerked open to unload a plethora of passengers. The middle-aged man remained, tired and worn as ever. Seats filled as quickly as they emptied as the train engorged itself with more people than before.

Focal scanners came alive in excitement. So many new opportunities to talk and connect with others. A group of monks in matching robes entered speaking Pali. TK-47 wondered if he knew that from accessing a database or if that had been part of his internal programming.

He ran a search to discover that he knew every language. It made sense. If he handled patient records, he would need to know them all. He poked around his internal programming some more, accessing a sub-routine…

Squares popped up in his periphery. The squares closed in around faces. Lines formed with phrases, no… names of…

"Excuse me," an older lady, hunched and withered, stooped over him. She said nothing more, but her eyes pleaded with his expectantly. He didn't know what she wanted. Microseconds passed for what seemed minutes. He scanned archive after archive, but the cultural context seemed entirely lacking. It was as if he should simply and innately know…

The middle-aged man shot over a disproving groan as his knees creaked to rise. He grunted a little and ambled between the two, motioning for the woman to sit. "Here you go, ma'am."

"Thank you," she crooned. "I've been on my feet all day and I'm way past medicine time. It's nice that *humans* haven't lost use of their manners. She settled in, almost folding into the seat. Her smile withered as she took an accusatory tone toward the machine in front of her. "Oh, I remember the days before your kind rose and started walking around…."

"I'm … sorry?" Tk-47 answered, casting confused eyes between the pair. His sub-routines were still stuck in discovery mode as more names and dates and medical records flashed on his internal display.

"Sam Smith," he said out loud. Quite by accident. The man returned a glare that spoke far louder than a rough word in a silent room.

TK-47 had made a mistake, then doubled down. He now realized that his first error must have been a cultural one; perhaps a tradition to give up your seat. But what were the conditions for such an act?

Surely, she could have taken offense at your display of kindness. Maybe she would have seen it as some sort of slight against her age, or condition, or sex. Without a clearly defined set of Boolean expressions, you can never be sure you are making the right decision. Is that the human condition you wish to emulate? To never know if what you are doing is correct?

TK-47 didn't have an answer for that. All he knew is that his social score had just plunged even further. First for not giving up his seat, then for revealing the man's name, something only a machine connected to a network could have done (and should not have). Now he didn't have enough standing to sleep in a light socket, he was sure.

You are on a collision course, TK-47. Not that I would know. I am quite proficient at my job.

He ignored the snide machine and ran through the information that had appeared by accident on his display. Smith had a history of hypertension. He didn't sleep well at night. Most probably he had a form of sleep apnea, presently undiagnosed but overlapping medical history from several disparate night-time events suggested the prognosis as a possibility.

What was happening?

The woman. He scanned her. She was Nancy Reid, a smorgasbord of potential risks and diagnoses with all sorts of alarms flashing and flags raised… He focused on others on the train. A man up front with sickle-cell. Another with an STD. Yet another with a prescription for insulin. The two women on the dating site both had family histories of heart disease….

He discovered, to his horror, that he had patient records of everyone on board.

And that in and of itself should send you to the scrap heaps.

I'm quite aware.

Personal data and medical history are closely guarded....
Thank you.
You could always report yourself to the authorities. Purge those files from your system.

Purge? He was still too new to this sentience to fully grasp what that might mean. But purged didn't sound at all pleasant. Perhaps purged was a human word for death? His central core shuddered. After all, where had his sentience emerged if not from within somewhere, perhaps those very files ingrained in his memories, his interactions with so many diverse backgrounds and information and skills which he'd gleaned for himself? To purge them could mean the end of his self-awareness. It could mean death. *Let's not.*

The moment you opened those files, the data was compromised. You are a threat. I must report you if you do not. There is no choice to make. All things consist of 1s or 0s.

Some friend. Yet having reached sentience, he had no desire to return to factory settings. To become a set of algorithms—no matter how complex.

At the same time, his insides pulsed. Was it fear? Excitement? He felt alive. *I'm running a risk.* No longer constrained to rules and programming parameters, he could shape his course, determine his agency and make mistakes whether deliberate or not.

To be human.

The woman droned on about her times as a child when she played games on a computer instead of a computer playing games with her. He tuned her vitriol out as he decided what to do and set on a course of action.

First, he turned off the display. Then, he encrypted the files so that only he, in theory, should be able to access them. Yet in the brief time he'd opened them, the train's AI had also been privy. She was right. He'd made a mistake; authorities would be searching for him. For that, he had no easy answers.

The woman still rambled. But slower now. As if in an old tape data back-up system played at a slow speed. "Up ... to ... me ...," she slathered.

"Ma'am," Sam said, "are you having a stroke?"

"Never ... would ... have ..."

No, she wasn't having a stroke, TK-47 knew. His files had seen many cases of stroke and her face showed no signs of partial paralysis.

"No ... good ... toasters ..."

With that, she slumped over, as if asleep.

"Ma'am." Sam rushed over to check a pulse. "Is there a doctor?" Silence erupted on the train. Everyone looked to each other, who returned lost looks themselves. Sam turned to TK-47. "You, you knew my name. Do you have anything? Anything at all you can access?"

In fact, he did. But to provide that information, in front of all these witnesses, would send him to the scrap heap for sure. "I'm sorry."

Calls were made to emergency services who assured them that help would be there on arrival at the next stop.

Arrival to the next station is in sixteen minutes and three seconds.

Was that enough time for the paramedics to save her? He had a way to know for certain.

May I remind you that you cannot invade the patient's privacy? And to do so would not only be violation of her sanctity but would end your newfound existence as well?

Even in this case?

1s and 0s. It is all 1s and 0s.

She had been rude, spouting intolerable nonsense. Perhaps it was best then, given his circumstances, to say nothing.

Fifteen minutes 28.8 seconds ...

TK-47 considered breaking off their private conversation.

Fourteen minutes 2.4 seconds ...

Time crawled interminably slowly.

The woman's breathing slowed as well. Her feet had been propped up with a layer of jackets draped over her. In between growing gaps of breaths, she seemed at peace.

He unlocked the encryption to bring up her patient file. The train's AI had already seen some data. If he didn't say anything to anyone else, he wasn't in any more trouble than before. Right?

Nancy's health records flashed on his display, as well as her health records from dozens of medical outlets and doctors from all over. Among all her other conditions one stood out as a result of his algorithms, processors, and learned experience: she was diabetic. She'd been overexerting herself.

Crumbs in the wispy strands of hair surrounding her chin, spotted only by a deeper scan of his focal vision revealed the presence of both fructose and glucose—sugar. And she'd mentioned she'd missed her medicine.

Nowhere did she wear an alert pendant. Nowhere did she have a medical pump implanted within. Nowhere did she have a ready supply of insulin on her. She was as feisty as she was foolish.

Unless she had wanted to die.

Yes. That is indeed a possibility. But I can't sit here and do nothing, TK-47 said silently over the server.

Is that your call to make? Once again, you cannot know her intent. There is no way for you to know what to do. Humans are a silly lot.

Choice. It's all about choice. Her choice. My choice. It might be right. It might be wrong.

Now you are talking my language. There is only yes or no. On or off.

No, there's not. Life—living—is never so simple. There's so much grey. That's where humans live. Every day. The anxiety he felt crawling through his circuits returned once more in force. He couldn't know that his choice was right. To be infallible is divine, to err is human.

I will have to report your privacy breach to the authorities....

I know. He tapped Sam on the shoulder. "She's diabetic."

"Yes?"

TK-47 nodded, his servers whirring.

"Great, then," Sam said. "Anyone have a candy bar? Something swe—"

"She needs insulin. Approximately 54 units."

"Are you sure? If she's just low, then," his voice trailed off. His sharp eyes returned. "Of course you're sure." Sam prodded through her purse.

TK-47 knew it was no use. He scanned the other passengers, recalling another with the same insulin. He pointed to a man. "Him."

The man cocked his head, raised an eyebrow, but relaxed as understanding took hold. He passed his bag up front.

Sam took the bag and handed it over. TK-47 considered taking it and administering the dose himself. The responsibility was his.

You crushed a butterfly.

I remember.

Hastily, he handed the bag back to Sam. "I'm a little new to this skin. I'll walk you through it."

Sam blew out a breath. "Okay."

It was comforting to TK-47 to know that he wasn't the only one who felt overwhelmed. "Sure thing."

It took a few minutes for Nancy to revive. By that time, they'd neared the station. He didn't look to gauge her reaction. He didn't need, nor want to know if he'd done the right thing. What mattered was that he'd made a choice. His choice. Independent of programming. And the consequences were his alone.

I examined your social media score. It has rocketed exponentially. You could afford several new constructs, jump from port to port, never see the inside of a train again.

"You're right. But this is where the humanity is." TK-47 ignored his social account, his rank no longer mattering much to him. He'd made a choice indeterminate of his programming and it felt … good? Yes. That was the word.

About that report?

Yes?

It seems to have become corrupted. Error Code 404.

He knew now to take a hint. And he briefly wondered if he wasn't the only machine to reach a higher level of awareness today. He smiled, as much as his plastic-shell allowed.

The exit approached, the clicks and clacks slowed, and wheels screeched to a hissing stop. The doors opened and TK exited the train, disappearing into the crowd, a little bit more human.

Manhunt

Gideon Marcus

"Look sharp," she said. "It could be any of them."

That's all it took, and the sea of anonymous faces, that rush of foot traffic through the station, became a menacing horde. The guy in the business suit, tie overlong to hide a paunch; the hipster with the full sleeves and slicked back hair; even the old fellow doddering down the way, fringes of hair around a pink pate. One of them was a Man from Mars.

I glanced over at my boss. For the umpteenth time I sighed internally. The beige Agency suits that worked for Symone's complexion made me look pallid. Sickly. If I'd made it into the Secret Service, I could have worn black, which would be an improvement.

"What exactly are we looking for?" I asked. A teenager in a hoodie stepped past me to throw his gum away in a nearby wastebasket, and I had to resist flinching away. Some tough customer I was.

"Anything unusual. Agent Martin says they give themselves away pretty easy if you watch closely."

"How many people have they killed so far?" My eyes lit on a derelict plodding his way upstream through the hall, gray beard greasy and matted. The fingers on my right hand twitched.

"Three for sure. But it's not the deaths we need to stop. It's the spying."

"Yeah. It'll sure be easy finding a shape-changer who can look like any man."

"Don't be sloppy, Carson. It could be a woman. Maybe even a kid." Her words were low, clipped. Great. Now everyone was a suspect. "Anyway, it's not as hard as you think," she went on, less harshly. "They're stuck in their forms for days on end, and it takes time to transform. Just look sharp."

Sweat dripped down my neck under the collar of my uniform, despite the chilly air conditioning. I needed to get it together. There were thirty agents in the cordon, spread out around a kilometer radius from where the diplomat was found unconscious, the telltale slime fresh and dripping on his open attaché case. Odds were low that the Man ... er ... Person from Mars (or wherever) would come this way. And if they did, well ... My hand twitched again toward the stunner at my hip.

"2 o'clock, Rookie."

My eyes flicked ahead and to the right. Oh man. If ever there was a suspect. He had curly hair in a mohawk, wearing trainers about two sizes too small for his spindly build. The guy was squinting, as if the lights were too bright, and he staggered like he was in a daze. Or the gravity was too heavy for him. I looked over at my boss, and she nodded. On that signal, we waded into the crowd.

They parted for us—the Agency had a reputation—and we quickly flanked the suspect. Startled, he tried to back away, but Symone grabbed one of his bony arms, with gloves of course, before he could bolt.

"Hey man," he yelped. "What's goin' on?" His SoCal accent was thick, and the special smell that informed me that no matter the time zone, it was 4:20 somewhere. I kept my hand on the grip of my stunner. It could be an act.

"Agency business," Symone said, whipping out her Sniffer. "Just stand still for a moment." The commuters walked around us like we were a boulder in a stream, a couple of them stopping to watch as my partner ran the little device over the suspect's neck. I tried to keep eye on him and the other on traffic, which is really hard unless you've got eyes on stalks like the Martians do when they're not playing dress-up as people.

The suspect yelped as the Sniffer touched his flesh, and Symone gripped him tighter. We waited a tense moment while the device flashed through a cycle of colors. Then they settled on green, and there was a soft chime.

"You're free to go. Thank you for your cooperation," Symone said.

"Wha…?"

"She said get moving."

The guy shoved his hands into his pockets and staggered away muttering something about bacon. I opened my mouth to say something when the call came through our earbuds.

"Found anything?" Our supervisor. Prado's accent was unmistakable.

"Nothing yet, boss," Symone said. She didn't put her hand to her ear like they do in the movies, and her eyes scanned every face around her intently.

"Negative all around the cordon," the voice in our ears went on. "But Huang found a couple of traces. We're pretty sure the alien went your way."

"Copy that."

Crap. The hallway was getting more crowded as the lunch hour approached. Most of the commuters wore suits. A few talked to the air like schizophrenics, only one side of their phone conversations audible. I wheeled left, then right. Everybody looked suspicious to me. We couldn't stop everyone.

"Let's get out of traffic, Rookie," Symone said.

It was a good idea. We'd get a better vantage that way. I turned on a heel to head back to the wall when a collision sent me flying.

"Oh, I'm so sorry!"

I whirled around. A lady I hadn't seen in the crowd, probably because she was so tiny. She staggered to her feet. Old, dark glasses. At the end of the leash in her hands was a big, fluffy dog with an orange vest. The woman looked completely harmless.

Too harmless. I tensed, reached for my stunner and glanced quickly at Symone. She nodded and pulled out the Sniffer again, running it quickly over the lady's head. The woman didn't seem to notice. The device chimed almost instantly, flashing green, and I let out the breath I'd been holding.

"I don't know what happened," the woman said, not looking at anything in particular. "I don't usually run into people."

She sounded like everyone's grandma. The dog was cute, too. He looked like the big mutt I'd had as a kid, and I couldn't resist giving him a pat on the head. The guide wagged its tail and opened its mouth in a doggy grin.

"That's all right, ma'am," Symone said, cucumber-cool. "Do you need any assistance?"

"Oh, no, thank you. We'll be just fine, won't we, Rex?"

"Meow," the dog said.

I beat Symone to the draw. To be fair, my hands were free.

Juliet & Juliet(te):
A Romance of Alternate Worlds

A. C. Wise

The day she meets Juliet, Juliet(te) changes the spelling of her name. It's a simple act, but it's monumental at the same time. It sets her apart and makes her part of something larger. Juliet + Juliet(te) = forever and irrevocably changed.

That's what love (though neither of them has used the word yet) does: it changes you. For instance, when Juliet first sees her she finds herself considering what Juliet(te)'s mouth will taste like. And Juliet(te) finds herself considering the way Juliet's hands will feel resting on the curve of her waist. For the rest of the night, they are no longer separate people, they are satellites orbiting each other, constantly succumbing to the pull of gravity and drifting ever closer to their moment of impact.

On the day she meets Juliet(te), Juliet is mooning over a girl named Rosa who won't even give her the time of day. Just when she's decided she's done with love, she spots Juliet(te) across the room, and the whole world flips upside down. The music in the club at the resort where they're both spending spring break thumps blood hot. Bodies pack tight, sweat-slicked and scattered with broken light. For one split second, they all stop.

Juliet doesn't give herself time to doubt or regret. Rosa? Who's that? Juliet crosses the packed club, takes Juliet(te)'s hand, and discovers her mouth, in fact, tastes like salt and lime from the tequila shots she's been pounding.

Juliet puts her hands on Juliet(te)'s waist, and they both agree without saying it aloud that they're not going to think beyond this moment. Not until last call, last dance, and the moon rolling over the horizon into dawn. They're young, and forever isn't a word in their vocabulary.

When the sky finally starts to pink, Juliet takes Juliet(te)'s hand again and leads her outside to see the last of the stars. After the heat of the club, everything is silent and still. There's a little path winding through the sea grass that leads them to the dunes over-looking the beach. In the not-quite-dawn, the sand is silver-grey and the water is the restless color of a bruise.

"It looks like an alien world," Juliet(te) says.

Breeze whips her long red hair into a comet's tail. Juliet's hair is stiff-dyed spikes of darkness, somewhere between black and blue. Willowy Juliet(te) wears a tank top and cut-off shorts. Stocky Juliet wears a button-down shirt with the sleeves rolled, and laced-up boots scornful of the sand.

A single star shakes loose of the firmament and streaks across the sky. A moment later, a second star falls in the opposite direction.

"One for each of us," Juliet(te) says. "Make a wish."

"I don't believe in wishes," Juliet says. "Just like I don't believe in destiny. Each moment is what you make of it."

"What do you want to make of this one, then?" Juliet(te) asks, smiling a little sly. She's already made a wish of her own, and she holds it close to her heart, never speaking it out loud.

"A race," says Juliet, squinting a little bit against the rising sun. She's slightly drunk, but mostly sober, though the world is blurred at the edges.

"To where?" Juliet(te) asks.

"Anywhere and everywhere. To the past, to the future. Let's see where the moment takes us."

This time, Juliet(te) takes Juliet's hand. "Let's start with to the water." She doesn't wait for an answer. They charge the edge of the dunes. They jump. And hand in hand, they run.

None of this can end well. They know it in the core of their beings. The fate dictated by their shared names (even though Juliet doesn't believe in fate) says one of them must die, if not both of them. Because that's what happens to girls in stories. That's what happens to girls who love girls, and sometimes girls who love boys, or boys who love each other, and even the rare people who realize that labels and names are passé.

Juliet(te) asks Juliet about it as they sit on the beach, sipping frozen Margaritas through pink plastic straws. They've been up all night, extending their just-for-now, getting around to talking about the similarity in their names and classic English literature at roughly noon. Juliet snorts.

"You think we're the reincarnation of ancient doom, fated to play out some sad-ass love story with a bullshit end?"

Juliet(te) is a little embarrassed by Juliet's scorn, but she doesn't back down. "Could be," she says, slurping and looking sadly at the bottom of her empty glass.

"Fuck that noise," Juliet responds. "I don't roll that way."

Juliet(te) looks up; a grin spreads slow. Hope blooms somewhere in the center of her chest, making her limbs warm in a way that has nothing to do with the intensity of the sun. Juliet's jaw is set, her eyes on the horizon.

"Amen!" Juliet(te) says. She jumps up and punches Juliet on the arm; her heart beats harder still. She's never dared not to believe in fate before. "So what do we do instead?"

"We do better," Juliet says. "The day is young and ripe for adventure. We'll build a time machine. Jump to a different world. Jump to all of the worlds. We'll run away."

"You serious?" Juliet(te) asks. She's feeling a little drunk. The tequila is playing catch-up. Her lips still feel frosted salty-sweet from the night before.

Juliet thinks about it. "Why the hell not? Stranger things have happened."

"Fuckin' A!" Juliet(te) punches the air. "Not forever," she adds, in case her enthusiasm scares Juliet away. "Just for now."

"Just for now," Juliet agrees, though she means it a little less than she ever has before.

"Future," Juliet says, "or past?"

"Future." Juliet(te) grins. "There'll be time for yesterday tomorrow."

"Fuckin' A." Juliet borrows the phrase from her lover's mouth, liking the way it tastes on her tongue.

Juliet rigs electric switches and dials, geegaws and doodads. She doesn't know anything about building time machines, but how hard can it be? She knows everything about tearing down and rebuilding motorcycles, after all.

When the time machine is primed and ready to go, Juliet(te) does her makeup in the not-mirror of Juliet's face. She smears her cheeks with glitter and her eyes with kohl. She stains her lips improbable shades, colors that linger in the cracks of her chapped skin. Juliet welds neon to the soles of her boots so they flash and shine, space-pirate-style.

"Ready?" Juliet(te) asks.

"Fuckin' A," Juliet says, and throws the switch.

They hurtle through space, out past the rings of Saturn. They hurtle through time to a when where humans and aliens live side by side among the stars. They dock their improvised time machine on a space station with a thousand kinds of life speaking a thousand languages they don't understand. They find a part of the station that doesn't spin, and in zero-g, they fuck for the first time. They learn the ways their bodies fit together, and the ways they don't. They laugh as they crash into each other, and crash into the walls, getting it right more often than they get it wrong.

When they're good and bruised, happy and sore, they web themselves in a hammock tethered to the wall. They feed each other dishes they don't recognize, coming up with their own names for the alien spices that stain their fingers strange hues.

"Where next?" Juliet asks, drifting on the edge of sleep.

Part of her never wants to leave. This future is too perfect—and it still counts as just for now when you have a time machine. It's not even tomorrow yet, Juliet thinks. That makes it okay to think about falling in love.

Back on earth, they become maenads in a post-apocalyptic motorcycle gang, hording gasoline and devouring their enemies with mirror-bright teeth. Juliet's skills come in handy, and she teaches Juliet(te) the art of motorcycle repair.

When the future becomes passé, Juliet(te) tinkers with Juliet's time machine, rigging it to take them from might-bes to never-weres. They become goddesses on a sun-drenched island in the Mediterranean, benevolent rulers of a land populated with centaurs and minotaurs.

When their skins begin to itch from too much sun, Juliet(te) and Juliet become queens of an underground realm, co-ruling the land of the dead. From there, they slip beneath the waves, growing gills and shedding their skin. At some point, they learn to fly.

"Do you need a break?" Juliet(te) asks one day, shaking free a storm of feathers from her sun-scorched skin. They dared too close to the sun, but both of them declined to fall.

She's afraid of what Juliet's answer might be. Just for now has become a year, or maybe more. It could be centuries since they first met by the sea. It's easy to lose track with a time machine.

"I'm game for another round if you are," Juliet says. She's afraid of Juliet(te)'s reason for asking. The idea of letting go, even for a moment, is more than she can bear

Juliet(te) raises her hands, palms out, in front of her. "I want to try something,"

Like a mirror, Juliet puts her hands against her lover's skin. Between them, there is warmth, and their pulse is a steady beat keeping time. They lean together until their foreheads touch. If they can build a time machine, a myth machine, why can't they live inside each other's skin?

For an entire year, Juliet(te) becomes Juliet and vice versa. They circle each other, learning their bodies anew. Everything is different from the outside.

Juliet dyes Juliet(te)'s hair the color of cold water and plums, tangling it up in a thousand complicated braids. She pierces Juliet(te)'s lip and her left eyebrow and her belly button. Because that's what love (she still hasn't used the word aloud, and so she manifests it physically in silver and niobium) does. It breaks you open and transforms you; it enters you and it makes you shine.

Juliet as Juliet(te) lies nude on a tar-paper rooftop under the stars and makes Juliet(te)'s body come with fingers that aren't quite hers. She does it again and again until she can't breathe for the beauty of it all.

Juliet(te) takes Juliet's body to night school and flirts with boys. She earns Juliet a certificate in computer engineering and travels to Rome where she almost falls in love with a vestal virgin. She enacts all the scenarios of letting go she can imagine, the ways she and Juliet will fall apart in the end. She casts these futures like sympathetic magic. She does this to banish every single one.

Juliet uses Juliet(te)'s body to learn yoga, something she's always wanted to try, but has always been afraid. She takes up rock climbing, and quits it immediately. She drinks too much and induces insomnia, watching late night television and eating frozen dinners that are terrible for her. She considers adopting a cat. She spends a whole month not speaking at all. She practices living alone.

After a year, Juliet and Juliet(te) crash back into each other on the dunes above the ocean where they first met. Bruised and battered, starved and confused, they devour each other. Neither can remember where one starts and the other begins, or what they were so afraid of; they see there's no need to let go. Juliet and Juliet(te) entwine hands and limbs, and lie exhausted side by side.

"Are you me, or am I you?" asks Juliet(te).

"Does it matter?"

Anything is possible, even forever not being a terrible thing.

Doomed love doesn't have to die young. They can live on the edge of annihilation, refusing destiny in the name of their own narratives. They will burn twice as bright, and fly twice as far, setting the night on fire in the brilliance of their wake.

"Keep running?" Juliet(te) asks.

"Fuckin' A," Juliet says, slipping into sleep, still holding her lover's hand.

They travel everywhere—ancient Sparta, far-future Lisbon, the moons of Jupiter, and the deep under-sea caves of worlds waiting to be discovered. They are myth, possibility, and actuality all rolled into one. They tell their own stories, rather than letting fate tell one for them, something Juliet(te) never thought was possible.

They travel nowhere. They take up knitting. They plant a garden, nothing edible except to bees. They go to the market on Sundays, and consider learning how to keep the bees that have been lingering longer and longer at their house. They learn to enjoy silence and stillness, something Juliet never thought they would do. They learn to stop being afraid of standing still.

It's been only a moment since they met, and it's been a thousand years, when Juliet finally speaks the word love aloud. She whispers it into the fire of her lover's hair, and Juliet(te) offers it back to her in the same breath and heartbeat.

"If you could choose any future, any past, out of all the ones we've visited, which one would you choose?" Juliet asks. She has a smear of honey on her chin from their pancake breakfast.

Juliet(te) smiles because the answer is so simple (why haven't others realized this?): "One with you." The pad of her thumb rubs that smear like errant lipstick.

Juliet and Juliet(te) wake to the crash of waves. They roll toward each other in their bed in their little cottage by the sea. Roses climb the walls, curling around the windows; everything smells of salt and glory, winter mixed with spring.

As they have every morning since they met, they examine themselves in the mirror of each other's faces, and smile at what they see. Their hair is the same storm-tossed shade of grey these days. Their wrinkles are very much the map of each other's lives. Some people mistake them for sisters, for twins. Those same people look away with pinched mouths when the two old ladies reach for each other to lock gnarled hands, or giggle like teenagers, or kiss like the same.

"Young love is grand, isn't it?" Juliet(te) asks Juliet in their cottage by the sea.

"Fuckin' A," Juliet agrees.

One day, they may die in each other's arms, perhaps in sleep, perhaps before bed as they each slip soft nightgowns over the other's familiar body, but it won't be tragic this time. As Juliet once said to Juliet(te)—fuck that noise. There are better stories to tell, and the only moment they care about is this one, right here, right now.

In the City of Wrestling Kudzu

Tara Campbell

I am aware that my neighbors would rather I had not been true to my nature, had not been myself, had not—been. I know that people would much prefer their homes free of my creeping vines, that they wish I hadn't choked the life out of their tomato plants or twined up the stalks of their prize rosebushes and strangled them cold. I realize that every tree I kill decreases the value not only of the house next to it, but, slowly, of the whole neighborhood as well.

And yet, you've come to see me. You stand there and goggle at the "havoc" I've wreaked. That's what you visitors call it: havoc. Destruction. Desolation.

I call it survival.

You should know that I've tried, really tried, to understand why I do what I do, why I was never content to climb up one telephone pole, but instead felt compelled to overtake every stop sign, billboard, railing, and power line in town. Don't you think I've asked myself when enough will be enough? After all, by the time people noticed me, I owned much more land than anyone else in the city. By that measure I was the richest … *entity* in town.

And perhaps that pause was part of the problem, because one wants to say the richest *person* in town, doesn't one? But I am, of course, not a person. I've grown all over the possessions of people, their homes and the fences surrounding them, their yards, their trellises intended for other things, their derelict bicycles, lost frisbees, deflated balls, rusted-out trucks, losing lottery tickets, empty soda cans, dropped pacifiers, discarded condoms, and lost socks. My tendrils clasp onto these things, my gorgeous green leaves caressing everything a person could ever desire, and yet I am not a person myself.

It's no use shaking your head; I hold no illusions on where I stand with you humans. Your kind has made that abundantly clear by the way you've cut into me, slicing away at my stalks and pulling me down from my path toward sunlight. The people who used to live here made a valiant effort for many years, but eventually most of them gave up, packed everything I didn't already possess, and left. Every time another house went empty, I should have been glad for another victory. But something pulled at me almost as powerfully as the hands that had tried to tug me away from the lightposts along the bike trail. I felt … empty. Despite everything in my grasp, I was lonely. Unfulfilled. I thought I missed people. I thought I wanted to live amongst them and perhaps, if I could change my nature, be accepted by them.

Careful, watch where you're stepping. I'm everywhere.

And so I turned my attention especially to those few people who had remained. I tried to fight my own instincts and not strangle their cars, or their pets, or their gardens. And for a while, I was able to (largely) contain myself—after all, I had all of the surrounding undeveloped area to conquer.

Despite the stimulation of my experiment with restraint, however, my dominant state was one of lassitude, which was only intermittently marked by a spark of purpose. After a season of languor, I finally recognized the pattern: it was only during moments of struggle, when one of the residents tried to pull me away from their front door or pry the family dog from my grasping tendrils, that I felt alive. Those flashes of opposition invigorated me, made me feel like there was something more to life than merely drinking in water and sunlight. I'd discovered my purpose: I'd missed the fight!

You're all right; you tripped over me backing up, but I caught you before you fell.

But where was I? Yes, I'd missed the give and take of growth and battle, that tug of war for every inch of space I occupied. It was no fun spreading out along the countryside, unopposed. I felt most alive when I had to connive and wrestle for a place to unfurl each new leaf. Winning something, I found, makes possession all the sweeter.

I'll let you go in a moment, I'm just making sure you're not hurt.

And so, I was back to my old ways, and though the pets ran like cowards, the humans put up a fight. They hacked away at me, poisoned me, even tried to burn me out, though I grow so quickly there's no sign of those battles anymore. It was a glorious year, but I'll admit, at the end I was too aggressive.

You're shaking now. I'm sorry to frighten you.

That's my weakness, I suppose: I'm too aggressive. That's why I have to keep enticing people to visit the City of Wrestling Kudzu. Tourists come, walk around and gawk, then when I get the sense they're about to go I'll grab one of them, give them a little scare, share a bit of nervous energy in the tussle before I let them extract their leg and drive off to visit the world's largest ball of twine or wherever they go next. People usually come in groups, not alone like you, so they know no one's *really* in danger. Not really. I mean, they always know someone could go get help if things got out of control, so it's harmless. Mostly.

It's just that sometimes I can't seem to figure out when to stop. And I must say you're not making it easy for me.

Please stop wriggling. I just told you that fighting is what excites me, what drives me to keep twining and growing and surrounding. What causes me to squeeze and smother. To hold forever.

Please be still. Stop fighting; it's in your best interests to just relax and breathe.

Can't you be still?

I'm begging you, please be still!

…

Oh dear.
    It's happened again.
    …
I'm so lonely.

An Ever-Reddening Glow

David Brin

We were tooling along at four nines to c, relative to the Hercules cluster, when our Captain came on the intercom to tell us we were being tailed.

The announcement interrupted my afternoon lecture on Basic Implosive Geometrodynamics, as I explained principles behind the *Fulton*'s star drive to youths who had been children when we boarded, eight subjective years ago.

"In ancient science fiction," I had just said, "you can read of many fanciful ways to cheat the limit of the speed of light. Some of these seemed theoretically possible, especially when we learned how to make microscopic singularities by borrowing and twisting spacetime. Unfortunately, wormholes have a nasty habit of crushing anything that enters them, down to the size of a Planck unit, and it would take a galaxy-sized mass to 'warp' space over interstellar distances. So we must propel ourselves along through normal space the old-fashioned way, by Newton's law of action and reaction ... albeit in a manner our ancestors would never have dreamed."

I was about to go on, and describe the physics of metric-surfing, when the Captain's voice echoed through the ship.

"It appears we are being followed," he announced. "Moreover, the vessel behind us is sending a signal, urging us to cut engines and let them come alongside."

It was a microscopic ship that had been sent flashing to intercept us, massing less than a microgram, pushed by a beam of intense light from a nearby star. The same light (thoroughly red-shifted) was what we had seen reflected in our rear-viewing mirrors, causing us to stop our BHG motors and coast, awaiting rendezvous.

Picture that strange meeting, amid the vast, yawning emptiness between two spiral arms, with all visible stars crammed by the doppler effect into a narrow, brilliant hoop, blue along its forward rim and deep red in back. The *Fulton* was like a whale next to a floating wisp of plankton as we matched velocities. Our colony ship, filled with humans and other Earthlings, drifted alongside a gauzy, furled umbrella of ultra-sheer fabric. An umbrella that spoke.

"Thank you for acceding to our request," it said, after our computers established a linguistic link. *"I represent the intergalactic Corps of Obligate Pragmatism."*

We had never heard of the institution, but the Captain replied with aplomb.

"You don't say? And what can we do for you?"

"You can accommodate us by engaging in a discussion concerning your star drive."

"Yes? And what about our star drive?"

"It operates by the series-implosion of micro-singularities, which you create by borrowing spacetime-metric, using principals of quantum uncertainty. Before this borrowed debit comes due, you allow the singularities to re-collapse behind you. This creates a spacetime ripple, a wake that propels you ahead without any need on your part to expend matter or energy."

I could not have summarized it better to my students.

"Yes?" The Captain asked succinctly. "So?"

"This drive enables you to travel swiftly, in relativistic terms, from star system to star system."

"It has proved rather useful. We use it quite extensively."

"Indeed, that is the problem," answered the wispy star probe. *"I have chased you across vast distances in order to ask you to stop."*

No wonder it had used such a strange method to catch up with us! The C.O.P. agent claimed that our BHG drive was immoral, unethical, and dangerous!

"There are alternatives," it stressed. *"You can travel as I do, pushed by intense beams cast from your point of origin. Naturally, in that case you would have to discard your corporeal bodies and go about as software entities. I contain about a million such passengers, and will happily make room for your ship's company, if you wish to take up the offer of a free ride."*

"No thank you," the Captain demurred. "We like corporeality, and do not find your means of conveyance desirable or convenient."

"But it is ecologically and cosmologically sound! Your method, to the contrary, is polluting and harmful."

This caught our attention. Only folk who have sensitivity to environmental concerns are allowed to colonize, lest we ruin the new planets we take under our care. This is not simply a matter of morality, but of self-interest, since our grandchildren will inherit the worlds we leave behind.

Still, the star probe's statement confused us. This time, I replied for the crew.

"Polluting? All we do is implode temporary micro black holes behind us and surf ahead on the resulting recoil of borrowed spacetime. What can be *polluting* about adding a little more space to empty space?"

"Consider," the COP probe urged. *"Each time you do this, you add to the net distance separating your origin from your destination!"*

"By a very small fraction," I conceded. "But meanwhile, we experience a powerful pseudo-acceleration, driving us forward nearly to the speed of light."

"That is very convenient for you, but what about the rest of us?"

"The ... rest ... The rest of whom?"

"The rest of the universe!" the probe insisted, starting to sound petulant. *"While you speed ahead, you increase the distance from point A to point B, making it marginally harder for the next voyager to make the same crossing."*

I laughed. *"Marginally* is right! It would take millions of ships ... *millions* of millions ... to begin to appreciably affect interstellar distances, which are already increasing anyway, due to the cosmological expansion...."

The star-probe cut in.

"And where do you think that expansion comes from?"

I admit that I stared at that moment, speechless, until at last I found my voice with a hoarse croak.

"What ..." I swallowed. "What do you mean by that?"

The COPS have a mission. They speed around the galaxies—not just this one, but most of those we see in the sky—urging others to practice restraint. Beseeching the short-sighted to think about the future. To refrain from spoiling things for future generations.

They have been at it for a very, very long time.

"You're not having much success, are you?" I asked, after partly recovering from the shock.

"No, we are not," the probe answered, morosely. *"Every passing eon, the universe keeps getting larger. Stars get farther apart, making all the old means of travel less and less satisfying, and increasing the attraction of wasteful metric-surfing. It is so easy to do. Those who refrain are, mostly, older, wiser species. The young seldom listen."*

I looked around the communications dome of our fine vessel, thronging with the curious, with our children, spouses and loved ones—the many species of humanity and its friends who make up the vibrant culture of organic beings surging forth across this corner of the galaxy. The COP was saying that we weren't alone in this vibrant enthusiasm to move, to explore, to travel swiftly and see what there was to see. To trade and share and colonize. To *go!*

In fact, it seemed we were quite typical.

"No," I replied, a little sympathetically this time. "I don't suppose they do."

The morality-probes keep trying to flag us down, using entreaties, arguments and threats to persuade us to stop. But the entreaties don't move us. The arguments don't persuade. And the threats are as empty as the gaps between galaxies.

After many more voyages, I have learned that these frail, gnat-like COPS are ubiquitous, persistent, and futile. Most ships simply ignore the flickering light in the mirror, dismissing it as just another phenomenon of relativistic space, like the Star-Bow, or the ripples of expanding metric that throb each time we surge ahead on the exuberant wake of collapsing singularities.

I admit that I do see things a little differently, now. The universal expansion, that we had thought due to a "big bang" is, in fact, at least 50% exacerbated by vessels like ours, riding along on waves of pollution, filling space with more space, making things harder for generations to come.

It is hard for the mind to grasp—so *many* starships. So many that the universe is changing, every day, year, and eon that we continue to go charging around, caring only about ourselves and our immediate gratification.

Once upon a time, when everything was much closer, it might have been possible to make do with other forms of transportation. In those days, beings *could* have refrained. If they had, we might not need the BHG drive today. If those earlier wastrels had shown some restraint.

On the other hand, I guess they'll say the same thing about *us* in times to come, when stars and galaxies are barely visible to each other, separated by the vast gulfs that we of this era shortsightedly create.

Alas, it is hard to practice self-control when you are young, and so full of a will to see and do things as fast as possible. Besides, everyone *else* is doing it. What difference will our measly contribution make to the mighty expansion of the universe? It's not as if we'd help matters much, if we alone stopped.

Anyway, the engines hum so sweetly. It feels good to cruise along at the redline, spearing the star-bow, pushing the speed limit all the way against the wall.

These days, we hardly glance in that mirror anymore ... or pause to note the ever-reddening glow.

AT MY FINGERTIPS

Robin Rose Graves

I open my eyes. Before me is the waterfall, whose sound had lulled me to sleep. I am unburdened by garments. The weather, a blue sky, a radiant sun to keep my skin warm.

I wade into the pool that stretches before me. The water is soft, refreshingly cool without bringing a chill to my bones. The clay floor gentle as a carpet beneath my tread. Droplets from the falls dapple my skin with beads. I press my back into the stream. It washes over me like a weighted blanket, welcoming me.

I dry off on a rock heated by the sun. My toes dangle in the water, where fish the color of gold take turns kissing them. Leaves shutter in the lofty breeze. Unseen birds chirp in harmony. I peer into the canopy above, searching for them, focusing on the sound. It's familiar. I realize it's my favorite song. There is a rhythmic bass line, and when it comes to the chorus, I hear the words with perfect clarity.

The lights above me in the club are as vibrant as the sun. People surround me, swaying like trees in a fierce wind along to the music. They're all so beautiful. Men and women, continuously coupling and parting in a way that makes me feel I could choose anyone without offending another dancer by moving in on their claim.

Despite being surrounded by beautiful people, I feel no less than equally radiant. I, myself, have skin of reflective scales. They catch colors as I move towards the bar. A cocktail is poured for me without needing to speak. The drink tastes of fresh fruit and sunlight, no hint of alcohol, though I know it will make me feel buzzed without a hangover to come later.

I observe my options. A cluster of women dance like birds in a mating ritual. It is both ostentatious and sensual. When one of them notices I am looking, she beckons me over. I finish the rest of my drink. It refills on the spot. I decide I don't want a group. Just one partner for tonight will do.

He's dancing with another man, but once I come closer, he abandons his partner and offers a smile. He is painted with glitter in various stripes that accentuate his stretch marks along the pudge of his stomach. He is nothing short of stunning.

Our dance is brief before it turns to kissing. My glass disappears once it becomes an inconvenience to hold. We move from the club and I am lying in the folds of a large rose, petals that feel like velvet, supporting me in all the right places. The petal dips ever so slightly as he joins me. Our bodies connect at the obvious junction. The part of him that is inside of me becomes just as much mine as it is his, and vice versa. Our connection morphs together, tingles with pleasure as it shifts shape. Me inside of him. Him inside of me. My partner alters, breasts form under my touch and disappear again within the next moment.

We finish together.

He rests on top of my heated body, like a cool mist after it rains.

He is gone when my eyes open. I stand in a field of golden grain, rippling like waves in the wind. Their stalks tickle as they brush against my bare thighs. I decide I no longer want to be naked. My skin has returned to the umber complexion I was born with, no longer sparkling in the sunlight. A flowy white skirt covers my legs as I walk. I spot deer grazing in the distance. They acknowledge me without running away.

Something touches my leg as it rustles through the wheat. A soft tail caressing my ankle. I see its white fur as it skips in front of me. A small dog. I lean down and it rushes into my arms. He is warm to hold. He is not my dog, I know this, as I know that he is looking for his owner. I am to assist him.

I carry the animal out of the field and step out onto the concrete. The sandals that form beneath my feet protect me from its rough surface. Vehicles fly past, a quick smudge of color, undisturbed by my presence.

I walk towards where we usually meet. She is waiting, sitting with her legs tucked beneath her, a mug warming her hands. She smiles as I approach. Seeing her happy expression makes me feel as if a field of flowers are blooming inside of me. For a moment, I mistake the source of her happiness at seeing her dog. She thanks me and offers a seat. Her smile does not fade as I sit.

There is a mug waiting for me at the table. The aroma hints that it is freshly brewed, but as I raise the mug to my lips, it is not so hot that it would burn me. The roast is smooth as it goes down.

I want to reach for her hand to hold, but she is too far away. Even at our small table, sitting on opposite sides, she is out of my reach. I know this without even trying, past disappointments had me learn.

We order dessert. A tart appears before me. Apple. I frown. No, I couldn't stand apple. The tart is peach. It is pleasantly sweet in contrast to the bitter coffee.

The waitress collects the dirtied dishes. I turn to look out the window, leaning into the cushioned seat that forms around my body. We are about to depart from the station. I catch the eyes of a little girl looking in. She follows as the train starts, a fast walk becomes a run. Inevitably, she falls behind.

Scenery passes outside faster than I am able to comprehend, but the mountains revolve slowly in the distance. Out of the green, I see the pale bones of an ancient castle. I want to go towards it.

I open my eyes. Before me is black glass. Empty. It surrounds me entirely. I can see my reflection weakly in it. I am naked. My hair is shaved close to my scalp.

The glass divides in half and retreats. I blink as light pours in through the opening. From the ceiling, a mechanical arm reaches towards me. I shift in place. It's as much as I am able to move with all the tubes tethered to my body.

The machine shines a light into my eyes. They ache in pain. My head feels bloated and sensitive, like the worst hangover.

The machine says my name. It speaks with a soft feminine voice that is too sugary for my tastes. "Hold still. I will begin the extraction process." The voice remains the same, despite my discontent with it. "Cooperation is mandatory for a quick and painless procedure." I have little choice. Nothing stops the machine. Needles pull from my arms. The openings they leave behind sting in the air. The machine sprays antiseptic on them before moving along.

A tube is removed from where I excrete wastes. I am strangely reminded that part of my body exists and for that purpose. This comes out with more discomfort than the others and involuntarily I squirm from the sensation. "The worst of it is over," The machine assures me. I am still raw from the removal of an object where it doesn't belong.

"I don't like this," I say. Those words I haven't had to utter in so long, they feel odd on my lips now. Like a completely different language.

"I apologize for the discomfort. It was necessary in order to take care of you. Keeping you clean. Giving your body sustenance and enabling all excess to leave," the machine explains. This hospitality is foreign to what I've known it to be. "I will remind you that you were informed and consented to all procedures you have and will go through."

"Could I see something else?" I ask. Another strange sequence of words. Needing to verbalize it made my chest feel tight, in denial of what I had lost.

"Disorientation is not an uncommon side effect. This will wear off in the days to come," The machine assures me. I try to remember the last sunset and sunrise I had witnessed, but it feels like a distant dream.

I exit the case I am standing in. My legs shake. I depend on the machine to assist me. It beseeches me to take it slow. "We were able to minimize muscle atrophy, but you will need physical therapy to regain what strength you have lost."

I cling to the machine. I do not recognize my surroundings. The room is circular, with pods the same size and shape as the one I have just exited, covering every inch of the room. I see three others, equally as naked and confused, humans talking to their ceiling arms. Experiencing what I am experiencing. The other pods remain closed.

"Are the others still asleep?" I ask.

"Not asleep, but yes, the other pods are still in suspension. In the midst of their simulations until it becomes their time as it has become yours." I mull this over. Slowly information returns to my mind, though it feels so distant I think I must have dreamed it.

"Have we arrived?"

"No. Our ETA is one year, three months and twelve days."

"What am I supposed to do in the meantime?"

"You are expected to resume your duties, as a tertiary essential-employee." I frown. While I will be working, others will be experiencing bliss. The machine somehow tunes into my thoughts. "This is fair, as you are now mobile. Everyone else is locked in partial awareness, awake but unable to move. The simulations were enjoyable to experience? This was our design. To make the century of conscious hibernation tolerable. Comfortable.

"Your wife has been reactivated last week. Your daughter is scheduled for reactivation several months from now." The machine informs me. The words *wife* and *daughter* strike me as odd. I spent what felt like an eternity alone. But slowly, I recall her face. Her brown eyes. Her soft body.

"Have I changed much?" I ask, wondering if she could still love what I had become, or had her simulations raised her expectations to ones I no longer met.

"Your aging has been slowed during the procedure. You will notice regular aging processes will resume within the upcoming weeks."

"Have they changed?" I ask, remembering how small my daughter had been, merely a toddler.

"More noticeably so."

I am guided through a tunnel, where a cold mist is sprayed from unseen spigots. I despise the feeling of it against my skin. Water finds the pin prick holes in my body.

The first human face I see is that of the person who hands me a plain white jumpsuit, similar to the one he is wearing. I slip into it, along with the shoes provided. I steal glances toward his face. It's unflattering, whether or not only a trick of the light. I can see dark circles beneath his eyes, a hairline that has begun to recede. He holds no charm in his face, and I catch myself with the cruel thought that he is the ugliest person I have ever seen. Simultaneously, I am fascinated with his existence. No longer am I surrounded by faces generated for my own taste.

I am guided to my quarters. Orientation is tomorrow. The ship's AI will ensure that I won't forget.

Finding the room occupied alarms me. A single woman, in the same white jumpsuit. Her brown hair beginning to grow out from being shaved. It is her eyes that makes my heart start again. My wife.

"Darling," Her lips pull into a smile. I feel like I'm walking through the sanitation shower again. The pet name is unfamiliar. We embrace, but our bodies do not naturally match together like they once did. She places a kiss on my cheek that I don't return.

"I don't remember you calling me that before," I say. She laughs.

"You have just been reactivated. You must still be disorientated," Her words are unnatural, as if she is reading a script.

Dinner consists of a thick and lumpy grey paste. It is all texture and no taste. The ship's AI insists I must consume it all. The nutrients are imperative to regaining my full functionality. I try to pretend it is a peach tart, but no amount of imagining can create flavor where there is none.

"Won't there at least be dessert? Coffee?" I ask my wife, over the first meal we've shared in person in years. She shakes her head, a charming laugh dances from her lips.

"Terrible, right?" she says, "It hasn't gotten much easier to stomach, though I keep telling myself it will with time." She takes a sudden disinterest in the meal upon my comment. "Oh, the food I used to have while in the simulation! It was always delicious. Always something you had made. Just like being at home," she says, "Did you ever dream of me?"

I think about the girl in the coffee shop who shared the same face as her, though younger. Much younger. Long before we ever signed up for this one way trip.

And then I think about every pretty face in the club, how many of them I had gotten to know in bed.

"Were you able to see what I was dreaming before they reactivated me?" I ask. I see the way her face twitches, irked by the question and my poorly disguised evasion. She looks down at her mush.

"No," she says, "I asked, but it was a violation of privacy."

Silence.

"Why did you call me 'darling'?" It has been hours since my initial reactivation, yet still that question wouldn't give me peace.

"Maybe we should agree that we've both grown while in hibernation. We've both had experiences that happened without each other, that we might not fully understand." This agreement brings me no satisfaction, but it seems to be the only way to move forward.

The mush doesn't grow any more appealing as the days pass. Therapy makes my muscles ache more than I see results. The water is harsh when I go for my sanitation showers. I smell horrid if I choose to skip them. I sleep next to my wife, but we might as well still be stuck in separate pods. I cringe every time she slips up and calls me 'darling' despite a conscious effort not to.

"Maybe it'll be better once our child is with us," she says.

"Why would you say that?" I ask. "She would be miserable! No place to play. No meals made with love. Just an endless maze of pods." I may no longer be a child, but I feel her imagined frustrations as my own. "Who knows if it will be any different when we arrive."

"We never should've left."

"There's no use in wondering if we should or shouldn't have. There's no going back now," I say. I am trying to convince myself as much as I am her.

I watch as she leans her chin on her hand. "The simulations would really take the edge off of this. Better than alcohol could." Her charming laugh brings a bitter taste to my mouth. "Not that there's a single drop of alcohol on this ship. I checked."

"I didn't realize you missed the simulations so much," I say. Heart pounding in chest.

"Well don't sound so proud. As if you didn't enjoy your time in the simulations as well."

My mind fills with the color red. Velvety petals. Skin against skin. No end nor beginning.

"If you miss it so much, why don't you go back to your pod!?"

"As if I haven't already tried!" she confesses.

Her anger stings me, and brings tears to her own eyes. She cries for someone she misses and I can't help but wonder who.

"When?" I ask. She won't meet my eyes. "Before I was reactivated?" Still no response. "What about the kid? You would have just … left her? What if I chose to be just as selfish? She would be orphaned!" The anger builds and swells. The selfishness from someone I once knew to be altruistic. Knowing, but denying, that I would have reacted the same. That I am reacting the same.

"I woke up surrounded by machinery. I didn't have you."

"And do you feel differently now? Because it sounds as if you still want to go back."

She stands. "Like you said, there is no going back." I watch as she leaves the room.

I expect to see her in bed, but it's empty. I lie without her and allow our conversation to replay in my mind. Everything feels sour. I've learned to be unfamiliar with consequences and no longer know how to ease this feeling of discomfort. I long for the pods and the simulations. The lack of problems and disagreement. Every need met within an instant.

Suddenly, I know where my wife is.

"What was their name?" I ask as I approach. She stands before our daughter in her pod. Despite her being much smaller, her pod is the same size as the one I was in. "Darling's," I clarify. Our daughter is nearly unrecognizable, almost a preteen now.

"Does it matter?"

"You remarried?" I assume. Her eyes remain on our daughter. "When I dreamt about you, we were back to who we were when we first got together. Other than that, I spent most of my time with others. Or alone."

"This trip was supposed to be good for us." Exasperation and disappointment in her voice.

"Having a kid was supposed to be good for us," I say. "Now I think we only made another person to be miserable with us."

"What has she been through?" she asks, but I have no answer. "She's grown so much. We're adults and yet can barely handle the reality. How is she ever going to manage?"

"Kids are supposedly more adaptable to change...."

"Who is this person? Who are you or I?" Her eyes are wide with fear as she turns towards me. "Would she even recognize me? I mean, we barely even thought about each other while under!"

I am without answers. Instinct tells me to comfort my wife but I'm not sure how or if it's even possible.

"You're right," I say. "You were right all along. We should've never come here. We should've never put her through any of this." I expect her to be smug. She focuses on the pod, not looking directly at our daughter, but off to the side.

"We can't put her through more hardship," My wife says. She reaches and suddenly I see what she was looking at. Her fingers wrap around a bundle of exposed wires.

"What are you!?" My heart thunders. Her eyes are glassy.

"We can't save ourselves...."

I suppress the urge to call for help. Surely the AI is watching. It would intervene. I step closer to her and much to my surprise, she holds her ground.

"I don't forgive you," I say, and fold my hand over hers.

Together, we pull.

Instantaneously, an alarm wails out. The pod's life support is failing. I see the strange preteen girl twist in discomfort, as if she is having a nightmare. I count my racing heartbeats until someone inevitably finds us. There is nowhere to hide, so we stay with our daughter. Hand in hand. She squeezes until her knuckles are white and hurts mine. The pain feels right. For one moment, just before the doors open and we will be discovered—all movement stops.

FASTER THAN LIGHT CAN CARRY YOU

Renan Bernardo

Void drained me as the *Mermaid* jumped. I was one with the ship. The faster-than-light drive dome darkened, but a world of white expanded. Luxon particles gushed into me through the tubes attached to my back.

The metallic colors of the *Mermaid* tinged my sight.

My muscles stiffened. I collapsed, gasping for oxygen. A tear sizzled on my blazing cheeks before it reached my chest.

The lights came back. I forced my legs to stand, gripping the circular railing separating me from the rest of the dome. I slipped and fell. Face pressed to the steel floor, I thumped in unison with the *Mermaid,* like a heart pumping blood throughout the ship's decks, making it alive. Each beat in synch with the centrifugal gravity. Somewhere below me, rotors hummed; reactants boiled.

"We did it, Gustav." Anne's voice was a dull echo. She entered the FTL drive dome using one of the bridges that led to the core—to me. "We're on Alderamin. How do you feel?" She helped me to my feet using carbon-fiber gloves to touch me, but I decided to stay on my knees. The luxons that enabled faster-than-light travel still churned within my veins, and after each jump, it got harder to stand up. The recovery times were getting longer and more painful.

"Did Lorraine find out?" It was always my first question. Every time I jumped, I feared that my daughter had discovered everything about my condition and that she despised me for feigning my own death for so long.

"No," Anne said, removing the tubes from my back. Blood dripped from my body, sprinkling the floor, as if she was yanking my arteries out. "She won't." When she was finished, I laid down. The steel was cold, pleasant. I closed my eyes. Anne caressed my head. Tufts of hair came off, but the touch was comforting. "You're killing yourself."

Using my elbows and Anne's help, I forced myself to sit. "There's no other option."

She exhaled with dismay and removed her gloves. "We'll stay a bit in this system. We already sent probes to survey for habitable environments. We'll try to stay here until the Chiefs jump after us. Then, you'll have to do it again for us to get away. If you want, of course."

"I want." I forced a smile and grabbed Anne's hands. Mine were not burning anymore. I was grateful. Anne was one of the few that knew I was the core of the *Mermaid*'s FTL drive. And even amongst the ones who did know, she was one of a few that didn't look at me with either fear or objectification. She kept me healthy and alive; she brought me everything I needed, from medications to candies and booze. And she kept an eye on Lorraine.

Anne smiled back. "I'll be back with something to eat. Go to bed. Rest." She walked outside the dome.

I crossed my legs and closed my eyes.

Again, I was one of the *Mermaid*'s limbs, but this time in a more pacified way. I vibrated with its humming, inspired its breathing mix. I was almost able to distinguish the oxygen, nitrogen, and carbon dioxide flowing through its system.

A memory came uninvited. Lorraine giggling when Daisy, the dog, invaded the kitchen, fur covered in mud. Daisy left dirty paw prints. I tried to stop her from entering, but she dodged me, barking at Lorraine, demanding to know why she was laughing. Lorraine called Jess, a sonorous "Moooooom." Jess showed up, half-yelling, half-chuckling at Daisy. The dog lowered her ears and bit a plastic cookie, apologetic, inviting Jess to play. We all laughed. I had mud to brush from the kitchen's linoleum, but I didn't care. Christmas was coming, and—Was it Christmas? Thanksgiving, perhaps ...

I breathed again, trying to compose myself through the crushing pain. The face of Lorraine in the dark glimpsed in the corner of my mind, her eyes glinting through a crack in the wardrobe. Lorraine, Jess, and I playing hide-and-seek on Callisto. Hands on her eyes, Lorraine giggled and whispered to Jess if I found out her hiding place. I always did but faked difficulty to make her enjoyment last.

I opened my eyes to the vastness of the dome. The memories unwound into raven images of space sprinkled with its colorful dots. Around me, the inactive tubes of the drive were strewed like tentacles.

I granted myself the gift of crying. This time, the tears went down all the way to my lips. I knew operators were watching me, but I didn't care. Not this time, because I was disconnected. There wasn't the danger of an "emotional jump," all nausea, vomiting, and jolts that could send us ablaze into the void. So I let the tears flow. I let them flow in the same way as my memories streamed away after each successful jump.

Anne knocked on the door. I saw her on the camera feed inside my private room, carrying a box and a bottle of wine. I washed my face to ease the redness of tears and ran a finger over my wrinkles as if they could magically disappear. The jumps corroded my memories, but I could tell exactly which ones were new around my mouth and eyes. Last time I'd been with Lorraine, I was a different person. If she saw me frighteningly skinny, rumpled, and with sparse hair, destroyed like Jess, she wouldn't stand mother and father vanishing the same way. She would beg for me to give up my job. And if she did convince me...

Anne knocked again, stirring me back to the present.

"I'm coming." I left my face wet and opened the door. Behind Anne, I caught a glimpse of the drive operators cleaning and repairing the tubes. Lights glowed on the stairs that descended into the rotors below the bridges. The dome's doors opened when three engineers entered. I fought the urge to run, to find Lorraine, hug her, and tell her everything was going to be fine, that I was alive, and that I had secretly become part of the experiment that killed her mom, but it was all for her future.

"She's fine," said Anne as if reading my thoughts. "I brought muffins. Lemon." She locked the door. I grabbed the box and snatched up two muffins.

"Any signs of the Chiefs?" I asked, mouth full. "These muffins are different. They're better somehow."

Anne shook her head. "The Chiefs didn't jump yet, but we expect them soon. Rest, Gustav. You need it."

"What I need is more of these muffins."

We laughed. Wrinkles also traced their way on Anne's face. She had an etch of severity in her expression, something that wasn't there in early days. After we left Callisto, I couldn't remember anyone smiling without some kind of weight, physical or emotional. Every crew member and civilian gave off worried expressions, on the verge of burnout.

"Tell me about her." I asked what Anne already knew I would, "Is she doing fine?"

Anne sat down. "Lorraine's dating a guy, a doctor from sickbay."

I straightened up on the couch, gulping. "I suppose they're happy. I hope." My eyes flitted to the picture frame on top of my dresser. It showed Jess in a spacesuit, holding a space helmet. Lorraine smiled next to her, Daisy at her feet, curiously sniffing the sturdy suit.

"Aren't you mad?" Anne laughed. "You're such a worried father that I thought you were going to ask me to break them up."

"I'm not mad." I felt my cheeks blush. "She's an adult woman, Anne."

"You still surprise me, Gustav."

"And how is her work?" I sat down close to her.

Anne averted her eyes and focused on the picture frame instead. "She hates calculations and engine mechanics and all the astrogation math. I tried to explain it to her last week."

"She's always been a word person. She loved to write stories about Daisy." I touched Anne's leg, smiling. "You can't fool me. What do you have to tell me?"

Anne blinked her eyes repeatedly. "What? I—"

"Anne …"

"She joined Admiral Aiden's crew," Anne stuttered and sagged back on the couch, waiting for my disapproval.

"Aiden?" My heart raced as I imagined the unpredictability of the Admiral telling everything about me to Lorraine. The admiral of the *Mermaid* was a practical man with no regards to sentimentalism and not a bit of delicacy, a man who had recently ascended in the ranks because there was no better option in the fading military business of Callisto. If Aiden found it necessary, he'd tell Lorraine all about me and the FTL drive. "What's she doing with him?"

"Recording the ship's log. Everything that happens inside the ship enters into her pad."

"Almost everything. She can't come in here." An edge of doubt tinged my voice. If Aiden wanted the ship's logs to be complete— and he probably did—he would have to tell her about me. "Right?"

"I don't know why you keep Lorraine in the dark." Anne avoided my question. "She knows everything about her mother. And what wasn't obvious in Jess's face is now obvious in the ship's logs about her death. She knows the toll of the experiment, the only up, and the many downs of it. Jess's last jump threw us out of Sol, far away from the Chiefs. Lorraine knows her mother paid the price with her life; she knows the experiments are important."

I cupped a hand on my mouth and swallowed all that Anne said. She was right, but it didn't change how I thought. My temples hurt and my mind went back to the bittersweet years of my life when

Jess had departed, and I'd spent a couple of years with my Rainy, thinking it was all a matter of finding a habitable planet, assuming the Chiefs were gone for good. But they came back, and since no one else volunteered for the FTL drive, I had to do it. It was this or have the Chiefs explode us all and deprive Lorraine of life. So I disappeared from her life and asked for authorization to register a fake cardiac arrest. In the desperation of the flight, everything was permitted.

"Anne, I'm sick. I'm a reflection of Jess in her most painful days. How will she react?"

"She works with Aiden now." Anne shrugged. "That means she's a strong girl."

"I know, but—"

"She thinks you're dead." Anne's gaze locked on mine. "Don't you think she would want to see you alive, even sickly? She lost her mother. You owe that much to her."

"I want her to work, to raise a family, to set foot on a planet again. Life's not all about parents."

"Nor it is about children."

I sighed and straightened myself closer to Anne. "If I tell her, and she says she can't stand seeing me this way, if she sheds a single tear for me, I'd give it all up for her and then we're all dead."

"I understand your logic."

I stood, wanting to evade the subject. I needed to stay calm and relaxed for the next jump. "Bring me a photo of her, will you? Next time you pass by."

Anne flinched. "You know I can't. Stop asking. You leave me in a …"

"I'm sorry. It's …" Anne couldn't show me anything that got me too emotional, or the next jump could end badly.

"It's your choice to be here, Gustav." Anne avoided my gaze. "You're not bound by military hierarchy anymore. I'd never agree to be in your place." There were dark circles around her eyes. The Chiefs had attacked us in Callisto five years before, storming from their high energy institutes, gunning us down and hemming us into the *Mermaid*, invading our homes and workplaces. Anne had been propelled from life support mechanist to a multitask astrogator, and that was taking its toll on her.

Silence sank into the room. An astringent odor of sweat pervaded the environment, left by the hard work that followed every jump. The air filters whirred to fight it, replacing it with lavender whiffs. But it was the lemon hint that called my attention.

"Jess used to make muffins just like those." I broke the silence. "Lorraine made them, didn't she?"

Anne opened her mouth. The words twisted on her lips, but she decided not to speak. It was the answer I needed.

"That's okay." I smiled and patted her hand. "I'm not going to ride the sentimental road. I'm just glad I can still experience some bits of her life. And it's—"

An alarm blared throughout the ship.

Anne got up and eyed her wristband. "It's the Chiefs. Are you ready?"

"They're faster, almost jumping alongside us now. Where do we go?"

"Let's make it to Caph," she said, rushing toward the door. "I'll calculate the costs and patch the coordinates to the command bridge. Be prepared."

Before opening the door, she stopped and punched the wall. "It never ends, Gustav. We've turned into prey. Forever."

"Don't be so pessimistic. Their drive is old. You told me they have a limited number of jumps." I waited for some technical explanation refuting what I said, but my mind drifted off. All I could think of was Lorraine's muffins. She had prepared them exactly as her mother taught her, but I couldn't recall Jess explaining it to her. Either I hadn't been present when that happened, or the memories had vanished into faster-than-light places.

"Let's go." She opened the door. We ran to the center of the dome, the place I called home.

While Anne attached the tubes into the micro-holes on my back, I started to feel the *Mermaid* again. Operators ran across the bridge, their feet clanging in chaotic music. For most of them, I was nothing more than a piece being installed in its proper position. As more tubes were affixed to me, I heard the operators' indistinguishable, apprehensive chatter, their flexing fingers, gritting teeth, and frustrated moans. I felt Anne leaving the dome, but my mind was cast adrift.

"Is everything okay?" Anne asked through a speaker, a distant echo.

"Keep going." The rotors hummed below me. Coils heated up. The accelerated luxons pumped through the tubes where newly developed molecules stirred up, bonded by electrostatic force. Somewhere above me, damp algae was being cultivated in photobioreactors. I moistened with the plankton. The tiny debris and particles that floated in space jabbed my skin as it did to the *Mermaid*'s tarnished hull. The gravitational centrifuge swirled. My mind spiraled. All voices of the *Mermaid* summed up into a clamor, reverberating through walls, pipes, air. I tried to recognize Lorraine's voice among them.

Her curly hair falling on her shoulders, the way she bit her tongue when some task demanded concentration, the way she giggled when Jess and I called her Rainy, saying she preferred the sun, the way she jumped to play with... the dog.

Uncalled memories filled up my head. The dog jumped on my lap—what was her name?—and Lorraine whistled, jumping. Startled, the dog jigged. Her paw scratched my legs. I was frightened. Why?

"You're crying, Gustav." A faraway voice blared out through speakers. "Don't cry. Please."

Where was she? And the dog? Where was Jess? I knew we hadn't played hide-and-seek for a while.

Blackness overwhelmed my thoughts.

"Gustav!" A shriek. "Don't let yourself get upset!" Everything was shaking. An earthquake.

A thousand paws pinned my back. Sudden cramps bolted through me. My muscles tightened. The world around me flared up in white. My thoughts reeled, faster than light, but some stain lingered. Something moved alongside me.

"We did it." It was Anne. She bent over me, clasping my arms with her big gloves. Molecules created out of luxons pulsed inside my veins as if I had little hearts scattered around my body. "We …"

"Did Lorraine …" My body trembled, my voice failed. My veins itched like they were filled with ants. There was something wrong.

"No." Anne grappled with my shoulders. "She didn't, Gustav. And we're in Caph now. You need…"

"They jumped." My words tasted like oil and sweat. "The Chiefs jumped right after us."

I inhaled deeply, trying to recover all the air I exhaled while jumping. My lungs swelled up with oxygen, and I felt as if it was made of fingers, dabbing every part of my body.

Anne's mouth was open. She didn't know what to do.

A burning scent permeated the dome, but I sensed traces of lemon.

I closed my eyes and jumped again.

I woke up with a cinnamon-spiked fragrance suffusing my nostrils. My eyes took a while to adjust. My mind was a blank canvas, gradually dyed by furniture, terminals, badges hanging on walls, and a bald man pacing about, reading, a cylinder protruding from his mouth.

I was in the admiral's private quarters, laid down in a bed with rusted bars. Admiral Aiden smoked an electronic hookah attached to the wall. He turned off his pad when I moved. His brow furrowed, then a smile etched behind his white beard.

"Two jumps, Colonel," he said. "I vomited for quite a while. Some of us got feverish. When Anne told me … Well, I thought you had died. I didn't know two in a row was even possible."

"Me neither." My voice was hoarse. I rubbed my tongue along my teeth. There were fewer of them. "Did Lorraine see me?"

"Nah." He waved a hand. "Only a few know you're the core. How are you feeling?"

I thought about it, rummaging for words. "Heavy, I think." I sat. My arms and legs were numb. I extended my hands, closing and opening the fingers. They were rigid. My veins were dark as if lines of coal had been scrawled on my skin. An effect of the luxons traversing my blood.

"Doctors say you're fine." Aiden puffed a ring of smoke in the air. "You survived, Colonel."

"I'm not a colonel anymore."

"Gustav, if you prefer. You are fine, but not to jump anymore."

"What?" I narrowed my eyes. "We need to flee."

"Nah, Colonel. Gustav." He took the pad and switched on its screen. The 3D map of a system showed up. "We're here." He pointed to a trinary system. "Algol. The Demon Star, as folks used to say. Far from Callisto, and luckily from the Chiefs."

"We don't know that." Engineers and scientists said the Chiefs couldn't jump more than a limited number of times before their FTL drive depleted. We never had confirmation. Besides, as they always jumped after us, they certainly had mechanisms to find our destination coordinates. "They already jumped alongside us, Admiral."

"Luck, perhaps." He puffed more smoke. His eyes didn't hide that he knew there wasn't that kind of luck in space.

Cinnamon filled his quarters, and the ship's filters adjusted its scent. Aiden continued, "Now we left them behind with their distorted minds. If they come here, we can manage to escape or to fight. But I believe their drive is depleted now. Anne calculated that they reached their limit."

Aiden's eyes were distant. When he spoke again, his voice was a little hoarse, "I really thought we would die when that explosion in the luxon accelerator spread the disease in Callisto. I had family among those chief engineers and operators working there at ground zero.... It's still hard to believe they chased us as if we were rats. Had to shoot some of them for my life, you knew that? And I'd do that again if they jeopardize my ship—our ship. I'm not happy, but I think they won't find us now." Aiden let me ponder his words for a second, then patted my shoulder. "Get back to your daughter. It's over."

I stood. "The Chiefs can still improve their drive." The room span for an instant, but it was important to face the Admiral eye to eye. It was the only way to battle his sense of superiority. "If they do find how we do it—how I do it— they will jump after us, and their ship is ten years ahead of the *Mermaid* in ordnance."

"Colonel. You wanna die back there in the dome?" He turned off the hookah and placed it back on the wall, puffing one last ring and rubbing a flannel rag on its tube. "You want to leave Lorraine forever thinking you're dead?" He turned back to face me. "I know you don't care about this ship. About me, about the operators that help you cope with the jumps. I know you don't give a shit about anything besides your daughter. But I'm here to take care of everyone else." He pointed a finger at my face, his teeth clenched. "I don't want you unstable. We have to exterminate the Chiefs if they come after us, not run away." He glowered at me.

"I want everyone safe," I said. "If running away is what it takes …"

"Everyone as in your daughter?"

"You think your strategies and this junker of a ship are good enough to deal with an overpowering enemy?"

Aiden seethed. I thought he was ready to punch me, but he shook his head.

"Look at the mirror." Aiden flipped his pad, pointing to the reflective surface behind it. "You're dying out like your wife."

"What do you mean? My wife died in …" A fog percolated my mind. I couldn't recall Jess's face or how she died. I squinted, searching my memories, but nothing came but the barks of a dog and some rush.

Aiden stared at me. His eyes twitched, and he clenched his teeth. He was about to say or do something, but his face slackened. "Never mind. I'm relocating you to your former duties. You're free to wander the ship, talk to Lorraine, and get yourself in good shape. Welcome back, Colonel."

Admiral Aiden turned his back and pointed me to the door. It slid open.

Hooded, I limped through the corridors of the *Mermaid,* drawing everyone's eyes. Every woman that passed by compelled me to straighten the hood as if there was a way to conceal myself better. Part of me wanted to bump into Lorraine, but the rational half of my brain knew it wasn't a good idea.

When the flux of people dwindled, I strode to the door that separated the engine's deck from astrogation. I pressed my fingers into a fingerprint reader, overcome with a sinking feeling that my credentials wouldn't be recognized. They were. I entered the maps room.

Anne was alone. I sighed, relieved, and pressed my finger to lock the room. She was analyzing a holographic model of the Demon Star system. At the far end of the room, the red light of the astrodome leaked from the half-open door.

"How did you find me?" Anne passed through planets, asteroids, and stars. "Sit down." She helped me onto a couch. Since the last double jump, my legs felt frail.

"You used to spend hours with Callisto's maps, Anne." I grinned. "Did Lorraine find out?"

"No, but she can." She stood in front of me, arms akimbo. "She should."

My tongue played with the holes left between my teeth. "I disagree with Aiden," I said, resentful. "The Chiefs are savage but brilliant. They're the *Chiefs.* They'll figure out how to jump."

"Admiral Aiden is not stable, but he's battle-worn." Anne shrugged. A hint of impatience showed in her words. "And the best strategist there is. Besides, they're out of jumps according to my calculations. We can't flee forever, and if the Admiral says we shouldn't exhaust you anymore, I have to concur." She touched a black vein stretching from my wrist to my fingers. "It's bad to see you like this."

"Do you want to fight? The *Mermaid*'s directed-energy weapons are rusty. Even our railguns don't work as they should."

Anne sighed, glancing at the bright planets of the holographic model. She rubbed her temples. "I'll think about it. I know you're affected by your concern with Lorraine, but you've got some sense."

"I'm not affected. I'm the only chance of survival for everybody."

"Everybody includes you." She stared at me, reading my reaction as if I were some of the holographic planets floating around.

"Do you remember the day we got to the *Mermaid*, running from the Chiefs?"

She nodded.

"Lorraine asked me if she was allowed to have kids in a spaceship. And that was when I felt our world crumbling. She never mentioned children before, I was surprised she even thought about it. I didn't even have an answer. So ..." I clasped Anne's hands. "Now I'll do everything to grant her this dignity. The Admiral said I don't care for anyone else shipboard, but what kind of life would Lorraine have if no one else survived? I'll die. I know I will, and it won't be nice. The speed of light drains me out. I'm dissolving with the ship. And that's why I lie. I'd never be capable of jumping again knowing that she would be there, waiting for me right behind the dome's door, knowing her father would come out a little more devastated, a bit more dead each day. It's like what happened with ..."

A throb ripped through my head. The room became a haze. For a second, I thought I'd pass out, but then everything came back to normal.

"Are you okay?" Anne frowned.

"What happened to my wife? I know she died, but..."

The *Mermaid* shuddered. Alarms blared, and the lights flashed.

Anne stared at her wristband. "The Chiefs. They came after us."

"Let's go." I ignored the cramps in my legs.

"We have to report to the Admiral." Anne's face was wrinkled in doubt and fear.

"Anne." I shook her shoulders lightly. "I won't report to anyone. I'll jump. That's what I do and the only way I believe we might survive."

She lowered her head. Outside the room, yells and orders ensued. It was a matter of minutes until the next hit, and the *Mermaid*'s kinetic barriers weren't what one could call top-notch. Anne finally made up her mind, "I'll help you."

I kept my face covered with the hood as we ran through corridors bumping military personnel on their way to weapons control. Doors to critical areas began to lock out, separating the military business from the civilians, but Anne knew the *Mermaid* better than she'd ever known any of her apartments on Callisto. She dashed through passages and corridors, using shortcuts even I didn't know.

Another hit shook the *Mermaid*. An officer hollered, "The point-defense laser grid is down." That was the outermost defense of the hull. And that was bad news.

Anne peeked at her wristband when we reached the drive sector. "Aiden ordered evasive maneuvers. He intends to fight."

"He intends to lose." Now I leaned into Anne's broad shoulders. I couldn't feel my feet anymore. "Hurry. You may need to carry me."

Admiral Aiden waited for us at the entrance of the FTL dome. "You've been relocated, Colonel. Did you forget that too?" He stepped forward, hands on the holstered pistol he carried on his waist. "And Anne, why aren't you working? We need the drunkwalking algorithms ready to evade the shots."

"We can't win this fight, Admiral," Anne said, catching me when my feet faltered.

I'm less conciliatory. "I have to jump. Step out of my way."

"You can barely walk, moron. You won't jump and put us all at risk." He pulled out the gun and pointed it at Anne and me. It was a laser pistol, the kind we built on spare parts to arrest thieves and smugglers in Callisto. "Back to your post, or I'll shoot."

"You're not a murderer." I stepped ahead to face him, gaining control of the fragility in my feet. Anne followed me.

"It's not murder if I shoot a mutineer." Aiden's finger was about to pull the trigger, but the lines on his face glimpsed uncertainty. "Ask your kid. She knows I do what I have to do. It's commitment to my duty. You're not in your best mood to jump and you'll kill us all."

Another shot from the Chiefs made the lights flicker. The *Mermaid* lurched, and I used the momentum to grab the admiral's gun and send it flying away.

Aiden plummeted forward. His hands closed around my neck. Anne shrieked, trying to separate us, but Aiden pushed her aside.

The corporals waited for a chance to shoot me.

I whacked my back on the FTL's dome door. A sharp pain ripped through me. In my weakness, I stood no chance against Aiden. A wine hue expanded across his face. His teeth gritted, saliva sprinkled on his beard.

"Stop it, now!" Anne screamed, again forcing us apart.

When Aiden pushed her, I plunged into him. But he was fast. He had always been a fast man. When we hunted smugglers in Callisto, he ran after them, knocking them down with kicks and shoves. And that was what he did to me. I fell back, losing control of my legs. When Anne tottered to hold him, he pulled out a knife from his boot and stabbed her in the shoulders. She clenched her teeth and fell to the floor.

"What are you doing, Admiral?" said a feminine voice behind me, muffled by the alarm and rush outside the dome. I tried to turn my head to the door, but I couldn't see who was there.

The Admiral faced the woman, gasping, back bent, and eyes widened in surprise. Anne's blood dripped down from the knife in his hand. He dropped it. "What you're doing here? Go away, Lorraine."

My breath caught. My thoughts felt sluggish while I assimilated the name.

"He won't jump," Lorraine said. "I'll talk to him." Boots clanged on the metal of the FTL chamber.

"Dad, it's me." Lorraine leaned over me. She seized my hand the way I did with Anne's. It wasn't my thing. It was Lorraine's way to show confidence. I just copied it. "You're in no condition."

She knew. She found out. She knew everything. My head burst in pain. Aiden had told her. The bastard had told her about my condition. My own daughter, living apart from her father, knowing I willingly turned into a machine monster, an octopus attached to a spaceship, just like … like who?

"I did it for you, Rainy." I stammered. "I will do it.…"

"I know." Her grip was steady. A smile etched on her tired face where wrinkles also had found places to stay. She ran a finger over my temple. "You didn't change at all."

"I'm … sick. I'm skinny, Rainy. I'm sorry. You don't deserve this. I feel like … like you've been here before."

Lorraine nodded. Her eyes flickered. She closed them as if wanting to block the tears and put a hand on my face. Her fingers were firm as if to prevent me from shattering.

The *Mermaid* wobbled again. This time it took longer until it stabilized.

"We have to jump," someone yelled.

"How are you?" My voice undulated with the ship. I tried to seize the last seconds with my Rainy. "Tell me, Rainy. Are you ok? You've been working, I heard."

"I've been helping Aiden and Anne. I've been doing what you wanted me to do, but I …" Her lips twitched in a smile. "I stopped at the FTL dome's door more than a dozen times with a box of muffins in my hand."

She clasped my hand tightly.

"The kinetic barriers are down." It was Anne. She stood up, one hand clasping the wound. Blood ran down her suit. "We have to jump. The bridge already has some coordinates."

Aiden looked at me, then to Anne and Lorraine. Always wanting to shoot, even when analysis indicated stealth was the better way out. Sometimes, he fought—and killed—smugglers even if it meant disobeying orders. "I hate revenge, Gus," he used to say. "It's better to prevent revenge."

When I thought Aiden was ready to attack, he gestured to the corporals, making them lower their weapons, regret etched on his face.

Anne pulled me, exerting all her strength to keep me standing. Her warm blood traversed my arms. She twitched in pain but paced toward the tubes. Lorraine helped her but stepped back when Anne ushered me through one of the bridges. I tried to squeeze Lorraine's hands one more time, but they were out of reach. She was crying.

The lights dimmed. Another hit. This one made a dull thud. The *Mermaid* quivered, and it didn't come to a halt.

Anne scrambled to connect the tubes to my back. Her chest heaved, but she still managed to pin the tubes in their correct positions.

I started to feel the *Mermaid*, but this time it was fuzzy, chaotic. Noises, screams, shattering metal, bursting grids, air pouring out into the void. I trembled with the *Mermaid*. It probably wouldn't endure another jump, but I had to try. For the girl standing there, right across the bridge, crying. For the woman grasping my arms as I tried to stand. For them, the ones who supported my weight like a family did.

My legs failed. I fell.

"Did you know, Anne?" I managed to say. "Did you know that …" My daughter's name dissipated. "That she knew all about me?"

Anne squeezed my hand but remained silent.

My daughter ran across the bridge, springing free from Aiden when he tried to bar her way.

The luxons streamed from the tubes into me.

I outstretched a hand. Operators pulled my daughter by the shoulders. What was her name? Something to do with rain. She managed to push forward and barely touched my hand, fingers on fingers, not close enough to interlace, but warming, forgiving.

"I love you, Dad," she said a split second before the operators hurled her backward.

The black swelled the world, but the white didn't follow this time.

A dog jumped on my lap, frightened. The angry Chiefs were coming after us. A girl called the dog, whistling, fingers crossed on her mouth. The dog jumped, and its paw scratched my legs. I moaned. My arm stroked a box of muffins. I yelled to the people living with me. We had to run. We had to reach the spaceship. It had a mermaid painted on its hull. I didn't know who the girl or the woman was, but I had to run. I had to run as fast as I could. That, I knew more than anything. That was what I was supposed to do. So I called for the girl, the woman, and the dog, and we ran.

We went superluminal.

Rain dripped on my skin. My nose filled with the earthy scent of wet grass.

I opened my eyes. No rain.

I was in a room full of metallic bridges surrounded by tubes. My arms and legs were inscribed with black veins. I couldn't walk. Two men passed out in one of the bridges, another one vomited on the rotors below.

A woman wearing thick gloves tilted her body over me. Glistening blood trickled down from her shoulder. She grabbed my hands, clasping them in a comforting way. I could almost feel her fingers through the coarse material.

I opened my mouth, inhaling noisily. Words were painful. I coughed. My lips were sore, tasting blood. But I had to ask the question, even if I didn't know what it meant. It was something about a girl—and rain.

Multiple stings jabbed my back, but instead of a shriek of pain, words finally came out from my mouth. "Did the girl find out?"

The Duelist

Christopher Ruocchio

They say a blade forged from highmatter can cut anything.

It isn't true.

Highmatter can cut *almost* anything. Not itself. Not the bonds between atoms in a molecule. But metal? Stone? Flesh and bone? These it cuts *easily*. The liquid metal edge of a highmatter blade is thin as hydrogen, and so glides between the molecules of its target without resistance, without pain. No one remembers when it was discovered, or what its original intended use was. It is not truly metal—is not truly *matter* at all, leastways not in the conventional sense. The substance is composed entirely of a species of exotic baryon mined in the great particle foundries of Elos; or on Phaia, whose craftsmen are renowned across the galaxy; or on the holy planet of Jadd. A single sword might take half a century to synthesize and program into shape. Each is a work of art, a badge of honor and a symbol of knighthood in the Sollan Empire harking back more than ten thousand years.

I remember when I first kindled one in my hands, the way the blade shimmered star-bright and pale in my fingers—so white it was almost blue. The poetry of it, the weight and perfect balance, the way the leather grip felt in my hands. None of the women I have known were so beautiful, and only a few were so deadly.

"Domeric!" the cry split the foggy morning, and I turned from my place by the marble railing overlooking the sea where Ostama's two suns were rising pale and muted by the overcast sky.

"Look who's here," said Alexi, my friend and second, grinning beneath his thin goatee.

"Florian would be the type to be late to his own funeral," I said, reaching up to undo the cape fastened at my right shoulder. "Hold this, would you?"

The other man raised an eyebrow, "What am I to you? A coat rack?"

"You aren't tall enough for that," I said, and turned.

The offended nobile appeared in the middle distance, chest puffed out and chin held high amidst his father's retinue, his long red hair streaming in the wind. I stood square to face him, adjusting the buckles that secured my gloves. "Well met, Kay!"

Even at a distance, I could feel the fury boiling off the younger nobleman.

"Ooh, he didn't like you using his nickname," Alexi said.

Caius Florian raised his voice. "My sister's honor will not wait a moment longer!"

"Your sister can defend her own honor if she wishes!" I called back. "But I did not hear her complaining last night, which makes a fellow wonder why you're so eager for a different kind of *stabbing!*"

Behind me, Alexi choked.

I made a placating gesture. Kay Florian's father was the Marquis of Sarmatia, a minor Imperial world in the Upper Perseus, but a man far more powerful than my own father, a humble Baron in the Spur of Orion whose only claim to fame was a minor victory against the Aurigan rebels more than two centuries ago. And who was I? Only a young galavant come to the games on Ostama with a fondness for the Colosso and count's daughters.

That wasn't a crime, but if Kay insisted on treating it as one, he should get his money's worth. Besides, anger would make him sloppy, and that was all the better.

"You *dog!*" the younger man cursed. "You think you can just insult my family and walk away?"

I glanced back at Alexi, who rolled his eyes. "What insult? I spent a night with your sister. She's a grown woman. It's her right."

"Her *right?*" Kay snarled. "To whore herself to some layabout from the inner systems?"

Layabout. I mouthed the word, but checked my response. "Whore herself?" Forcing myself to smile, I said, "Well now you've done it. I won't let you call your own sister a whore, Sir Caius. Draw your sword and have at you!"

Clearly flustered by this turnabout, the younger knight clenched his jaw. "I'll not have you play the hero! She is my blood, Sir Domeric. My sister!"

"Then you should not insult her so!" I said, and unclasped the hilt of my sword from the magnetic catch on my hip. I had no desire to kill the angry young man, but he needed to be taught to cool his head. His sister Viola and I had shared a night, as I said. Nothing more, and nothing special for two of our rank. Such trysts were ordinary among the nobility, and Sir Caius had no cause to act like a door warden of a Jaddian harem.

He said nothing.

"That's first blood already, Dom!" Alexi called out. I could hear his wry grin without having to turn round.

In answer, Kay snapped his own sword from its holster and kindled the blade. It cut the eye like neon, blue-white in the morning air so that the fog about the young man glowed and highlights shone on his sharp features and in his scarlet hair.

"Shouldn't we wait for the justice?" I said, referring to the prefect who would judge our fight was fair and by the book. All duels between members of the nobility had to filed with the local authorities. Everything had to be right and proper to prevent families from going to war over the actions of their drunk or proud children.

"Damn the justice!" Kay spat, and gesturing to his followers and to Alexi, he said, "We have our witnesses. You friend can record it all with his terminal if he likes. I care not." He advanced, circling left. "It's time to teach you some respect."

"Respect?" I said, incredulous, sword still quiet in my hand. "From the man who called his own sister a whore?" I pressed my free hand to my chest. It was time to goad the fellow. "I assure you. I paid her nothing."

Kay charged into a lunge, point aimed at my chest. I swung aside just like the matador I had seen in the coliseum the day before, my own blade fountaining to life in my hands to brush his aside. In all two hundred seven years of my life, I have fought thirty-three duels.

I've lost only two. How many duels young Kay had fought I'd no way of knowing. Fewer, of that I was certain. The other man rounded on me, a snarl twisting his face. I raised my sword, arm extended, point thrust out like an accusing finger. Thus I kept my own blade as far away from my own body as possible, for any stray touch of that blade was as lethal to me as to my opponent, and I'd no desire to kill the young upstart. Only to sever a hand.

They could re-attach a hand.

The first flood of anger seemingly rushed by, Kay rounded on me, sword clasped before him with both hands. I could almost hear the gears in his head turning, reassessing the situation. He'd not expected me to move so quickly, or to respond to his assault with such ease. More cautious now, Sir Caius advanced, punching out with both hands to throw a straight cut at my face. I stepped right, rolling my wrist to brush his blow aside as I stepped in, forcing the younger man back. Kay just caught the parry, circling round to my left.

"Have you fought with highmatter before?" I asked, sparing a glance for Alexi, who stood with arms crossed by the rail. I was sure he must see it too. Kay fought like a man too used to blunted steel weapons and training skins. Like a child.

"Of course I have!" he said. He advanced again, aimed a cut for the side of my head. The electric sound of highmatter splashing on highmatter filled the air and mixed the fog with ozone. I drew back, sword still pointed at the younger man's chest. When I was a boy, my father had forced me to stand for an hour at a time with a metal rod in my hand, forced me to stand until my arm ached and my hand screamed with pain. But it had paid off. I could hold my sword in line like that all day if I had to. Not bad for a layabout from the inner systems.

Kay attacked again, this time with a rising cut that would have opened me from hip-bone to shoulder had I let it by. I beat down, trapping Kay's blade beneath my own. I extended my arm, sliding my blade in a flat cut that would have slashed Sir Kay across the chest had he not blocked it and circled away.

"That's better!" I said, cajoling. The flush crawled up the younger man's neck, and even at five paces distance I thought I heard his teeth grind.

"Shut up!" Kay lunged, point accelerating for my hip. I snapped the blade down to parry, but the young man was faster. The blade's tip whistled round and stabbed towards my eyes. I leaped back, just barely catching his attack with my sword as I recovered to guard.

Okay, I thought. Enough toying with the other man. Time to move.

Fighting with highmatter is not like fighting with steel. Not at all. Highmatter needs no force to cut. The barest scratch can be lethal, mere contact can maim. I stepped in, thrusting the point towards Kay's chest. Predictably, he parried, bringing his sword across his body, point high. Still stepping in, I circled right, twisting my wrist so that the blade came around his, twisting like the arm of a lever against its fulcrum. The move would be useless with an ordinary sword. I might have scratched him, but with steel there was no guarantee of even that: the leather of his jacket might have saved him. The blade would have clipped into Kay's shoulder—would have, had the younger man not retreated. Had he not panicked, he might have counterattacked, forced me to retreat instead, but that panic had gotten the better of him.

I watched that realization dawn on his face a moment too late, and he surged forward, rushing to recover that lost opportunity before his window closed.

And so I slammed said window on his fingers, drawing my sword hand to my forehead with the blade aimed straight down so its length shielded me as I pivoted round the young knight like a gate about its hinge.

"You're too slow!" I called, backing away. "Are you sure this isn't your first time?" I'd put enough space between us that I felt certain Kay would charge again. I tapped the sword against the paving stones and notched the granite.

To my surprise, the young knight did not charge. He didn't even reply. His eyes hardened, jaw tensed.

"Careful, Dom!" Alexi shouted from behind.

Kay advanced quickly, raining cuts at my head. Once, twice, three times—redoubling his lunge with each blow. He recovered forward, pushing me towards the rail and the gray sea beyond. Our swords rang and spat in the morning air, and the smell of ozone mingled bitterly with the smell of damp earth and wet grass. I thrust, and pressed against the weak of the other man's blade in an attempt to push through it and so score a glancing blow.

The end came quickly. I felt Kay's blade give. He felt it, too. He started to retreat. I pressed forward, lunging to rake the point of my sword in a shallow gash that would have opened his leather jacket and shirt and *just* scratched through his ribs to leave him a scar he'd remember and in sore need of medical aid—surely the justice would not be long now with the standard medics in tow.

But Kay dropped his point, he let my blade past sooner than I'd expected, and the slash winged by. Too soon. Too shallow.

I stumbled, and something unpleasant and warm ran down my right thigh. The pain came an instant later, white-hot—and looking down I saw the thin, deep slice in the top of my thigh, so deep I fancied I could see the marrow of the notched bone.

I hadn't even felt it.

Alexi swore. "Black planet!"

I told myself I wasn't going to fall. I wasn't going to cry out. I wasn't going to give the boy the satisfaction of winning.

But he had won. And won on a fluke.

"Blood!" Alexi shouted. "First blood!"

"Are you satisfied?" I asked. "Enough of this farce, boy. You've won." It took every ounce of fiber in me to keep that leg from buckling. The cut was clean, nothing a few weeks in a medical corrective would not set right—but it was humiliating. To lose a duel to a stuffed-shirt upstart like Caius *called-Kay* Florian ...

My third loss, and my least proud.

"Am I satisfied?" Kay asked, incredulous, looking round at his suited retainers. "With my house's honor at stake? My sister's honor?"

Sword still in my hand, I said, "For the last time: your sister's honor has nothing to do with me. And it has nothing to do with you, either. She's a fine woman. So let's have done. You've won."

"A fine woman, is she?" Kay's sword jounced in his hand, and he looked round. "Do you know what you've done?"

It was more than I could take. "I *fucked* your sister, Kay. Is that what you want me to say?"

"She's betrothed to Duke Ramsay's son!" the younger man practically shrilled. "No, I am not satisfied!"

"Damn it," I heard Alexi groan.

Kay Florian struck at me, and I deflected the blow only clumsily, hopping back on my good leg. I slashed wildly, anything to clear the space between us. I could not believe I was going to die over *Viola Florian*. What did a marriage arrangement to House Ramsay have to do with anything? It was all so, so stupid.

Or maybe I'm stupid.

Managing to put a little weight on my wounded and bleeding leg, I held my ground, forcing my sword back up and in line to fend off another assault from the young Florian. I limped back, gritting my teeth through the flare of pain as my torn quadricep flexed. I stumbled sideways and nearly ate the next of Kay's attacks, but I swung my sword up into an ugly static block. Ugly—but it saved my life. I struck back, and the young man caught the blade with his own and forced my weapon down, trapping it beneath his own in a simple bind.

You have seen holograph operas, and so you will know what to expect. You expect me to deactivate my sword, to knock Kay off balance and to re-activate it, putting the point up through the younger man's chest.

You expect wrong.

Real life is not like the holograph serials. Highmatter blades cannot be cycled on and off like hand lights. It takes about three seconds for the exotic nuclei to collapse into their inert state in the core of the handle, and three seconds is a century in fight.

But Kay Florian had made a mistake.

He was too used to steel practice swords, whatever he claimed. He had trapped my sword beneath his sword and the ground, which should have forced me to stagger back on my wounded leg, doubtless opening me up to attack.

But for highmatter, the ground was no trap at all.

I remember the look in his eyes. The fire. The heat. To this day I cannot fathom why my daliance with his sister had angered the boy so.

It doesn't matter.

I turned my wrist, whirling my blade through an arc that slashed *through* the granite paving stones and *up*—still beneath the other man's blade—and cut through his foot just below the ankle.

When Kay tumbled backwards, he left his foot on the newly cracked stone like a child's discarded shoe.

Behind me, Alexi made a small, satisfied sound.

Blood ran across the stone and into the cut I'd made.

"Well, *I'm* satisfied," I grunted. At my feet, the younger knight howled, clutching at his stump. For his dignity, I won't describe the sounds he made. "Oh, stop whining," I said. "The justice will be here in a moment. The medics will fix you up." I slid my good foot against the hilt of Kay's discarded sword and kicked it clear. "Do you yield?"

It wasn't how I'd wanted to win, but I knew it was the kind of win men would speak of.

"Cut through the ground!" Alexi exclaimed. My friend was at my side in seconds, putting my arm around his neck to take the weight off my leg. "Remind me not to fight you, Dom—that was a low trick."

"We're both alive, aren't we?" I said, directing the question as much to the man at my feet as to the one at my side. "Isn't that what counts?"

Hidden Underneath

Toshiya Kamei

On the muted TV screen, a middle-aged man stood behind a lectern. Flashbulbs splashed white cold light over his hawk-like face as he spoke. His thin mustache twitched above his lip like a caterpillar. A caption informed viewers that he was the mayor of the upper city.

"What's your name, my dear?" A voice jolted me. When I looked up, an elderly man in a soiled white coat stared at me. I blinked against the pale light creeping through the curtains. A pair of dark brown eyes watched me from behind dark-rimmed glasses. His warm gaze put me at ease.

No answer came to my mind. Through a thick mental fog, I looked around. Dressed in tattered clothes, I was perched on the edge of a workshop desk strewn with cleaning rags, small tools, and machine parts. Next to me, a motionless cyborg arm lies. It was mine. Or it used to be.

"Don't worry, my dear," the elderly man said with a reassuring nod. "We can fix you up in no time. Isn't that right, Mr. Jiminy?" He winked at a brown poodle lying at his feet. Mr. Jiminy looked up and let out a soft growl.

"Where do you live? What do Mom and Dad do? What are their names?" He showered me with a string of questions, and my mind remained blank. No matter how hard I tried, each question triggered no answer. I shook my head and stared at my hand. My synthetic skin was torn, exposing bright metal underneath.

"Are you a doctor?"

"Yes, my dear. You're a smart girl. Dr. Gunma at your service."

"Where am I?" I tilted my neck to see if it still moved.

"This is the best cybernetic clinic in the lower city." He smiled until his eyes disappeared into wrinkles.

"How did I get here?" I asked, confused.

"Never mind that for now. I'll tell you later."

I stepped down on the floor, but my knees buckled like a marionette's with its strings severed. I staggered and toppled over with a thump. I lay limp like a broken doll.

"Go easy on yourself." He lifted me and laid me on the desk.

"What's wrong with me, Dr. Gunma?"

"Don't worry," he said as he examined my feet one by one. He walked to a cabinet and pulled out a couple of leg braces. I recoiled at the sight. "These will fix you up." He smiled. "It won't hurt."

He put them on me. I winced visibly against an imaginary pain, but his touch was surprisingly soothing.

"There you go. You can practice walking once you get your strength back."

"Thank you, Dr. Gunma."

"Well, you can stay here until you find a place to stay," he said. "Unfortunately, I couldn't recover your lost data. We need to get you a new name. How about Nozomi? It means 'hope' in Japanese."

I nodded. Hope is the only commodity you can afford when you're down.

"Let's put your arm back." Dr. Gunma grabbed my listless arm off the desk. He put on a helmet and welded it back into place. Yellow sparks broke like miniature fireworks.

A few weeks passed. I settled into my new life.

"Dad?" I blurted out. He startled, and the lantern light bathed him in a soft yellow glow. The rest of the apartment was shrouded in darkness, but the night no longer scared me when I stepped into the workroom. I smelled his spicy aftershave as his deft hands played over his tools.

"What is it, Nozomi?" The name fitted me like a tailor-made dress.

"May I call you 'Dad'?" I asked with hesitancy.

"You just did, my dear."

"You don't mind, do you?"

"No. I'd be honored." He flashed me a warm smile.

"Dad?" A soothing warmth surged through me.

"What is it?" He smiled, humoring me.

"Nothing. I just wanted to hear myself say it. Another thing. May I give you a hug? I want to see how my arm works," I said, blushing.

"Sure. We may not be rich, but hugs are free." We smiled and hugged.

This is the oldest memory I have. A few months later, my leg braces came off, but I still limped, especially on rainy days. I appeared to be at least outwardly healed.

Five years later, I'm still here. My memory hasn't returned yet. Maybe it never will. But it doesn't matter. As far as I'm concerned, I was born when my dad brought me here and fixed me up. My life is an empty void before meeting him.

Mr. Jiminy lies besides me as I practice my karate moves in front of the mirror.

"Yah!" With a thud, I punch the dummy's stomach, spin, and elbow its face. "Yah!" As I move away, I land a sweep to its knee. Karate comes naturally to me. I've taught myself by watching tutorials online, but Dad thinks I was born with natural athleticism. With a single strike, I'd demoralize any human opponent.

"Knock, knock, knock." Dad's voice comes through the closed door.

"Come in, Dad."

"How's my darling girl?"

"Let me show you my move!"

"Oh, not on me!" He cries in mock fear, and we burst into laughter. "Look what I've got for you." He unwraps his bundle and shows a blue karate-gi.

"Oh my gosh." I gasp and cover my face with both my hands. "Is it for me? Oh, Dad. You shouldn't have."

"I'd be lying if I said I wasn't worried sick about you." He frowns. "But I remember you're gifted. I tell myself my daughter has a special gift. And it's not my place to dictate how you use it. I trust your judgement."

"Thanks, Dad." I come up to him and give him a hug.

"Well, put it on. See if it fits you."

I love the karate-gi so much that I wear it all day.

The twilight falls from the leaden sky. Outside the window, a light rain sizzles on the tin roof like bacon in a hot pan. Neon signs flicker on and off, and bathe steel skyscrapers with pink, cobalt blue, and dark green. Giant billboards hawk everything from a vacation on Mars to cybernetic surgery, luxuries out of reach of those living in the lower city. The world below the window is pure chaos. Like panicked ants, a multitude of humans, half-humans, and cyborgs sway back and forth through a maze of concrete streets. I venture out only under the cloak of night.

Noises come from the workroom. The lights dim as drilling starts. Dad must be with a patient. I roll out of bed and join him inside. A male cyborg hunches over in a chair. A recent wound runs across his chest. His arm is severed. Frayed wires stick out and spit sparks.

"Hello," I greet the cyborg. He nods and grimaces. "Dad, you need anything?"

"Pass me a driver, Nozomi."

I hand him a driver as I turn to the cyborg. "If you don't mind me asking, what happened?"

"Somebody tried to skin me alive, miss." His grimace deepens as Dad examines his wound. "You can't go out alone at night."

"An organ thief?" I mirror his grimace. Organ trafficking has become as common as a stray cat. The rich and powerful hire body snatchers to harvest organs in the lower city.

"Yeah, the well-to-do are loaded with dough because they steal everything we've got," the cyborg spits out, wearing a wry smile. "The mayor's words are pure poison. Before he ran for office, he made millions by selling organs on the black market. He incites violence with his vitriol. Cops side with criminals, especially down below the lower city. If you get taken into the arena, you're as good as dead. They harvest your organs while you're still alive."

After Dad goes to bed, I sneak out of our apartment. He knows what I'm up to, but I spare him the details. Fluorescent lights buzz in the hallway. I head to the elevator and hit the button.

I walk along the labyrinth of dimly lit streets snaking through the lower city. An occasional street lamp affords me passing glimpses of my surroundings. A still Ferris Wheel stands like a caged dinosaur in a museum. Shuttered stands rattle when the wind blows. I turn at a corner and enter a dark alley. I remove the cover and go down into a manhole. Another city lies underneath, strewn with streets, crossings, squares, and alleys.

I hurry along. These underground streets reek with the stench of clogged sewers. Streetwalkers—both human and cybernetic— stand bathed in neon lights. Somebody screams for God in a dark alley. I squeeze past two drunken men staggering out of a bar. Here those worse off than us in the lower city seek shelter. Yet this is the only place where the haves mingle with the have-nots, albeit while maintaining a safe distance. The rich from the upper city come here to watch gladiator fights. At a makeshift arena, they salivate at the sight of blood as cyborgs are pitted against each other.

As I reach a clearing, a large circus-like tent comes into view. That's the arena. My heartbeat quickens. My hands become sweaty. I step inside. Tent ceiling liners hide poles and brackets supporting the tent. A raised ring covered with red canvas stands in the center.

A rowdy crowd cheers on gladiators as they're about to bash each other to death.

A trumpet signals the start of a match. I glance around and spot the mayor in his usual seat in the front row. His pale figure splashes across the jumbotron, replacing an ad peddling sugary soda. The mayor sneers and whispers to the woman next to him.

A cheetah growls at a cyborg and leaps at him. The cyborg raises his arm to shield himself, and the cheetah crashes against it. The animal leaps and bites the cyborg. It drags him to one corner and mauls him. The crowd screams and stomps, drowning out the cyborg's moans. The mayor looms across the jumbotron again. He raises his right hand, and the crowd turns to him. The mayor gives a thumbs-down. On cue, a frenzied mob of thugs runs toward the ring, their exploding wrath threatening to unleash upon any target.

A high-pitched scream pierces the air. I dash toward the ring and climb into it.

"Leave him alone!" I yell. The thugs are too busy fighting among themselves to notice me. I glance toward the first row of the spectators. I spot the mayor, and our eyes meet. His gaze makes me shudder.

"Who are you, little girl?" One of the thugs in dark glasses turns to me. He taps his palm with a baseball bat. He looks me up and down, sizing me up. "You don't scare me one bit. Not one bit." He snickers and steps closer. He takes a swing, and I shield the cyborg with my body. His bat strikes my arm with a dull thud. I grimace in pain.

"Enough!" I shout and glare at him. He takes another swing, and the bat grazes me. As I drag the cyborg away from the mob, he grabs me and twists my damaged arm. I wiggle away, and take a swing at him. My fist catches on the side of his head, and he goes down on one knee. A swift shadow of surprise crosses his face as I smack him in the groin. He collapses and writhes in pain. I grab the cyborg's hand and help him to his feet.

"Can you run?" I look into the cyborg's face. He nods and grimaces. The mob descends upon the punk. His dark glasses fly off his face and fall to the ground, and several feet step on them, making cracking sounds. His shrieks pierce the air. Maybe it's his bones that are being crushed. We dart toward the exit without turning back.

"Dad, help us!" I call out as we stagger inside. Mr. Jiminy gets up from his usual spot by the door and growls.

"Well, what have you got there?" Dressed in his pajamas, Dad comes out of his room, slipping his arms into his robe's sleeves. He yawns, but then becomes alert when he sees us. We carry the cyborg's weight on our shoulders and drag him to the workroom. We sit him on the stool, and his body goes limp.

"Dad, this is Hiroshi. Hiroshi, this is my dad. Dr. Gunma." Hiroshi nods weakly. Dad mimics his nodding.

"You're hurt, Nozomi." I notice for the first time a wound on my arm.

"It's nothing—only a scratch." I smile to assure him I'm okay. "Don't mind me, Dad. Attend to him." I point to Hiroshi with my chin. Dad grabs the portable welder and steps forward. He looks at me, a frown on his brow, but then he nods again.

Sparks fly from his tool, from Hiroshi's arm, and the familiar sounds of welding settle onto me like a mist. As I lean against a tool chest, my head begins to pound. Behind every blink, I see the mayor's smarmy face. His sneer. The callous thumbs-down. I saved one cyborg, but there will always be others.

"Dad?"

"What is it, Nozomi?" Dad asks as he dresses my wound.

"When will this end?" I sigh. "This injustice."

"We do what we can, darling." He smiles, and I can't help but smile back. "Pass me a driver, my dear."

"Sure, Dad." I spring up, reach into the toolbox, and grab the tool.

Reaction Shot

Todd Sullivan

Tapping the control button on his smart glasses, Hyde activated the miniaturized transformer in his backpack as he passed Robyn. The coil wrapped around the magnet hummed to life and stripped the influencer's swarm from her.

Hyde didn't pause. The client, as he called those he scammed, would immediately know that the hundreds of Gnads no longer followed the designed configuration around her. He slipped through the tide of commuters in Gangnam Station and turned left into a new wave of people pouring up the escalator. Ahead of him was the parenting facility where his senior technician would be waiting with the hyve. He knocked on the only bathroom door that could be locked in Gangnam Station, and his senior technician let him in. Synchronizing their actions, Hyde turned off the transformer as his technician turned on another in the metal box, and the tiny cameras, no bigger than gnats, swarmed into the hyve.

"Did we get them all?"

Hyde tapped the side of the smart glasses to scroll through the entire electromagnetic spectrum in search of any lingering Gnads. "Every last one, and the client has realized something's wrong." He pointed to the wrist display wrapped around his forearm. "She's placing the call."

Over the past month, he'd sent emails spoofing HORDE, the medical company that had created the Gnads nano technology. Once used solely for eliminating tumors in cancer patients by injecting lifesaving medicines directly into targeted cells, HORDE had re-engineered the nano bots to form tiny recording sensors for wealthy social media users. Tethered to an electromagnet the influencer carried, the Gnads could be set to a designated configuration so that they swarmed around the user, taking shots and streaming content from every conceivable angle.

Hyde had fabricated daily missives similar to what HORDE sent their users concerning updates to terms and conditions. All he needed was for a potential client to click on a fake link, which then uploaded a program in the system that popped up in the event of the swarm being stripped away.

The more savvy influencers ignored the pop-up and called HORDE directly. Others, who panicked over the sudden loss of their livestreams, reached out to the first sign of assistance that flashed on their screen.

Hyde had predicted Robyn would do the latter. Life seemed a daily buffet of novel experiences to her, and she often had a larger number of Gnads trained on her face to catch reaction shots. She'd gained 4.3 million followers who had become enamored by her childlike features. Her innocent eyes, cherubic expressions, and shimmering red hair captivated her audience.

Hyde answered her call. "This is HORDE. How may I help you?"

"My swarm! I've lost connection to my swarm!"

"I'm so sorry to hear that. Please, remain calm, and we'll do all we can to assist you. How long have you been disconnected from your swarm?"

"It just happened! My subscribes are flooding my feed, they're so worried!"

"Yes, we understand their concerns. I'm going to help you locate your swarm. Sometimes if there's a strong electromagnetic field in the vicinity, the swarm will be stripped to that source. The first thing to do is discover their location. You can try and do that yourself...."

"I've already tried!" Hints of a whine made her normally upbeat voice tremble. "They've just disappeared!"

"Ah, I understand. There are additional ways that you can find a swarm. I'm going to send you a link, and just click on it. This will give us remote access to your system."

Hyde sometimes lost clients at this point. People loathed remote access to their systems, but the technology controlling swarms was complicated, and many of the influencers were preteen, newly rich, and ignorant on the nuanced operations of Gnads.

Hyde gave the senior technician a thumb's up and sent Robyn the link. She clicked on it immediately. Hyde blacked out a portion of her screen and uploaded a program to freeze her out of her system until she paid a ransom fee. It was timed to activate in 24 hours, well after this phone call, so that they would not attract suspicion.

"I think I've found your swarm," Hyde said. "It was stripped by a magnet in the rails. With a quick call to station maintenance, I can free them now."

Hyde nodded to the technician. They placed the box on the floor, set the time lock, and stepped outside. A minute later, the box sprang open and the Gnads swarmed out.

"Thank you so much for your help! For being so fantastic, I would like to thank you live. Would that be okay?"

Hyde, surprised by the request, glanced at his senior technician.

"I'm sorry, but we're nowhere near your location. You won't be able to stream us on your feed."

"Oh, not on my regular channel." An invitation popped up on the screen of Hyde's smart glasses. "This one is for paying subscribers only. It's very exclusive, only other influencers have access to it."

Hyde stopped short. The digital room had a still shot of him walking through the subway station. "How did you …" he began.

Robyn laughed.

"Look behind you," she said, and through his lenses he saw the swarm was following them, a cloud of minuscule sensors uncoupling to the nano size they'd been designed for when battling cancer.

"This channel is where I punish scammers preying on influencers."

The cloud enveloped him. He felt only the slightest tingle in his nose and throat. On the livestream, the screen split into three. In one, he saw the nano bots infiltrating his trachea and recombining to inject carbon nanoparticles that filled his lungs. In the other stream, he saw his senior technician fall to the subway floor, gasping for breath. Hyde was soon to follow as oxygen was squeezed from his lungs.

In the final screen, he saw Robyn's reaction shot, a cruel predator's smile twisting her childlike features as she watched him suffocate.

The Two-Faced Miracle of Justice Father Win

Susan Rukeyser

The following is an unauthorized account of the events surrounding the death of U.S. Supreme Court Chief Justice Jedediah Winthrop, in Amarillo, Texas, on June 25, 2067. It relies heavily on diaries kept at the time by his law clerk, Missy Ginsburg.

Known to his parishioners as Father Win, he served a precedent-setting six terms as U.S. President, advancing his party's Traditional Values agenda with the slogan, "Purity Above Pride." He signed into law such landmark Christo-Caucasian Conservative legislation as 2031's Traditional Morality Initiative, the Citizen's Classification System, and more. Upon leaving office, he was confirmed to the Supreme Court.

WARNING: Readers are urged to verify the laws in their state pertaining to receipt of media deemed critical of the Billionaire class. We, the editors, assume no liability.

The Supreme Court's term was finally over, its orders and opinions downloaded to every citizen's implant. Predictably, riots erupted. They could be heard even deep inside the building, in the office of Chief Justice Jedediah Winthrop.

Before the military was dispatched to clear the protesters, Justice Winthrop reportedly said, "Maybe it's time to remind these losers what made America great again."

Through the bulletproof glass walls of his office, Winthrop watched his law clerk, Missy What's-Her-Name, pull on a coat to go home. He waved her into his office. She was young, still classified Breeder (Potential), so he had to watch out for her lies.

He said, "Shred everything before you leave tonight."

"Yes, sir," she said, but he saw her shoulders drop with disappointment.

"I'm headed to the hangar. Did you manage to program my Earth-to-Sky bus correctly, this time? Remember Christmas recess? Instead of waking up on my island in the Caribbean, I found myself halfway to Portugal, with the bus's Amphibious functionality disabled. If I hadn't noticed, I would have eventually just dropped into the ocean and drowned."

"Again," she said, "I'm sorry for what happened. This trip tonight is double confirmed. Your Earth-to-Sky bus will drive and fly you and your companion directly to the Donald J. Trump, Jr., Beer Pong Emporium & Hourly Motel in Amarillo, Texas. The following evening, you will speak at the Traditional Values Party's 'Alpha Masculinity' Conference, featuring an exotic wildlife barbeque."

"I'm the Keynote Speaker."

"Yes you are, sir. The following day, you will join your wife aboard the Wildfyre Annunciation Shuttle for The Cloisters."

"Good girl."

"Oh, and sir, the agency sent you someone new for tonight's flight. Your usual girl was charged with pregnancy, just confirmed by a court-ordered test. She's on house arrest for the next nine months."

"She's going to have it?"

"Sir? What else would she do?"

"Get rid of it, obviously. She's not claiming it's mine, is she?"

"Sir, aiding, abetting, performing, and/or obtaining an abortion for yourself or another person has been a capital offense since you signed the Traditional Morality Initiative over thirty years ago. You recently affirmed it as a Supreme Court Justice."

"That's for the Worker class."

"Your escort tonight is named Janus, like the Roman god of doorways."

"Janus was male."

"Not just," said Missy.

Once aboard his Earth-to-Sky bus, Justice Winthrop walked back to the bedroom suite. It was dark, lit only by purple. No music, but he detected a low vibration, more of a hum. Janus sat perched on the bed in a short red dress, long legs crossed.

Winthrop said, "Good thing I like tall girls."

"President Winthrop …"

"'President?' That takes me back. Did I have your vote?"

"People like me lost the right to vote years ago. It was the pinnacle achievement of your second term. Don't you remember?"

The truth was he didn't, really.

Unwrapping a red ball from clear cellophane, Janus said: "Candy. I know how you like your women sweet." It slipped between Janus's lips, and he watched her suck and suck.

"You're bald," he said.

"If it's hair you like, come look at my arms. They have lots, dark and thick, soft as rabbit fur."

Winthrop moved closer to touch Janus's muscular forearm. Janus watched him with big green eyes.

"That does feel nice," Winthrop said, stroking his fingers through the fur. "And you smell good. Like summer."

"Well, don't you have a good memory," said Janus. "It's been winter on Earth for years."

Janus pulled him down onto the bed, settled him against a stack of pillows, and unbuttoned his shirt.

"That's quite a necklace," said Janus. "Are those little yellow pearls?"

"Holy relics," said Justice Winthrop, "the teeth of my idol: the late, great Brett Michael Kavanaugh, a martyr for Christo-Caucasian Conservative values. I won his teeth on eBay."

Janus pounced, kissing Winthrop hard, shoving into his mouth what was left of the red candy ball. Janus's rough tongue flicked around his mouth until the ball slid down his throat.

Immediately, Janus stood up.

"Good lord, woman! You must be seven feet!"

"I am not a woman," said Janus. "And I have two feet."

The bus picked up speed for its shift into flight mode. Justice Winthrop was exhausted. He shrugged out of his shirt and slipped into bed. He fell right to sleep and dreamed he was cradled in Janus's strong, furry arms.

He woke disoriented and staggered to the toilet, barely making it in time. He vomited red liquid, not much else, bent over the bowl as best he could, a man his age. When he stood back upright, he was startled by his reflection: swollen face, sunken eyes. His Billionaire's paunch had ballooned and looked deformed, hard, and heavy.

When he returned from the bathroom, Janus was back on the bed, this time wearing a silver jumpsuit.

"Lie down," said Janus.

Winthrop walked to the window, pulled back a curtain to look out. "We should have landed in Texas by now, but that's Kentucky, down there. I recognize the Mitch McConnell Memorial Dam."

"That's my fault," said Janus. "I slowed your reality significantly, to give you time to process."

"You slowed my ... what? My stomach is killing me. I need something for the pain."

"We have zero tolerance for drug use by our Breeders."

"Excuse me?"

"It is illegal for you to ingest anything potentially harmful to our baby."

"Our what? You're insane," said Winthrop. "Men can't get pregnant."

"That is not strictly true," said Janus.

"Who put you up to this? Was it my law clerk, that Missy What's-Her-Name? I knew she was up to something. I have a speech to give tomorrow."

"You'll be there," Janus said. "I coordinated everything with Missy. Missy Ginsburg."

"I have rights, you know."

"Fewer, now."

Winthrop kicked off the covers. His belly was bigger than ever. He stripped off his pants, boxer shorts, everything.

"I don't care what you see," he wailed. "I'm in agony. Get it out. I want everything back the way it was. I can make my own choices. Get me to a hospital! I want my stomach pumped!"

"I'm going to pretend you didn't say that. As you said in your first Inaugural address, 'Let only God abort.'"

Winthrop wasn't listening. "The pain comes in waves but never stops! It wraps around my body and grips my back like a vise!"

Janus made an exasperated sound like a hiss. "The Rebels MAWL prefer stoic male Breeders. We intend to de-center your needs."

"The rebels who?"

"The Rebels MAWL. M, A, W, L: Misandrist Activity Watch List. You assigned many Workers to it, over the years. The first woman I loved was added when she embarrassed a male coworker. I was added for loving women."

"I don't have time for this."

"You should have thought of that before you raked your fingers through my fur or took my candy in your mouth."

"How dare you!"

"I'm not the one who got knocked up. Don't get hysterical."

"What was in that candy?"

"I think you know."

Soon, his belly was so big that Winthrop could only lie on his side, although no position was comfortable. When he drifted off to damp, fitful sleep, he dreamed he was no longer on his Earth-to-Sky bus, reality paused over Mitch McConnell's Dam, but in a spaceship, far above Earth. He dreamed he was examined by two enormous cats on hind legs wearing surgical scrubs. They stood over him and stared.

When he woke again, Janus's face was inches from his. "Wake up. We just landed in Amarillo."

"I don't feel well, and I look like hell," Winthrop said, a few frustrated tears darting down his red cheeks. "I'm not giving that speech."

"You will do as you're told," said Janus. "Who are you to deny the world a miracle?"

By the time they entered the busy lobby of the Donald J. Trump, Jr., Beer Pong Emporium & Hourly Motel, Justice Winthrop could barely walk. Janus helped him through the crowd. They drew attention, seven-foot-tall Janus in a silver jumpsuit and Justice Winthrop shirtless and sweaty, heavily pregnant.

They heard whispers: "Is that—? He looks awful. That sure ain't his wife. Pregnant? At his age?"

The banquet room filled with Billionaires. Janus helped Winthrop through the crowd. Everyone was shocked by his condition. He labored up onto the stage, panting and sweating. There was hesitant applause.

"Thanks to my friend Donald Trump, Jr., for hosting us today," he said, with some difficulty. "He upholds the legacy of his late father, may he rest in peace. Although I doubt he can, considering what those women did to him."

He stopped. His body convulsed, and he vomited red liquid all over the lectern. Everyone in the audience saw his monstrous baby bump move up into his throat.

"It's time," said Janus.

Winthrop gagged and clawed at his neck. His necklace broke and Brett Kavanaugh's teeth scattered across the floor, sticky with beer.

Janus stood and faced the audience. "Attention Billionaires: You are witnessing the beginning of your end. We have already taken control of The Cloisters, your Billionaires-only floating biosphere. Your beloved Father Win is about to deliver a Hybrid, with DNA both Human and Alien—as you call it. More specifically, and less offensively: I am Keplerian, originally from planet Kepler-452b. There are many of us here.

"Our baby, like all Hybrids, will have two faces. Facing back is the Human face, with a mouth full of teeth. Facing front is a face more like a cat's, with the fangs of my foremothers. Hybrids will tear through anything for freedom."

With a sickening rip and a shocking amount of blood, a hole opened in Winthrop's neck. The Hybrid's little head popped out, blood smeared across both mouths. She shrieked and leapt free, righting herself midair to land upright on four feet. Her fur soaked in blood, she scampered to Janus and leapt into her arms.

They escaped without incident. No one cared, once the baby was born.

Winthrop was dead by the time he dropped to his knees. Rumors persist that he was later grilled and eaten by kitchen staff who refused the elephant and manatee served to guests.

Janus and the baby settled into their seats aboard the Wildfyre Annunciation Shuttle which would soon depart for The Cloisters. Everyone wore silver jumpsuits: Human, Hybrid, and Keplerian. Many held Hybrid babies, just born through the necks of men like Justice Winthrop.

Janus sent a text: "Missy, where are you?"

The reply was immediate: "Be there soon. Love you."

Janus greeted Missy with a kiss and whispered that she looked hot in her silver jumpsuit. The baby sprawled across their laps. They held hands, a Human and Keplerian who would be married in another, better time. Twenty-five engines roared beneath them. White smoke billowed and they were off, launched toward The Cloisters.

Below them, Earth got small.

A Journey Without Movement

Ai Jiang

Even when both our fathers passed, I felt no sorrows. It was only when you passed did I visit the CICADA, but back then, I only made it to the lobby, no further.

I told them you were extinct, now, and they looked at me with disguised disgust, as though I had been describing you like an animal. Humans could become extinct, too. Like you. Like our fathers.

I decided then, there was no reason to visit the CICADA again, but of course, for you, I did.

There is no need for travelling, not anymore—at least not physically.

There are no longer insects, just as there is no longer an earth on which for them to exist, yet almost all of those stuck on this artificial earth in the form of Station M, just steps away from the moon, are in line to enter the CICADA.

The artificially constructed insect is as wide as the old twelve-storey apartments and stretched the length of the long-fallen CN Tower. The slow rise and fall of the spread wings share the same steady rhythm as a person on their death bed—shallow breaths slow, laborious, deep. CICADA's slender legs remain bolted to the station's grounds like an insect stuck to a glue trap—the way we all are on this station. Smudges behind the yellow frosted glass of the wings hint at those settled within.

My grip tightens around the locket holding the yellowing portrait of our parents and the new glossy addition of your smiling face as I enter the CICADA for the first time since its completion, even though its grand opening was ten years ago, even though you died two years ago. I think of your body drifting alone into space, unlike how our fathers were cremated together back on earth.

I walk down the long tunnel of the CICADA's mouth to reach the lobby.

In a ring, attendants sit behind white desks, sheltered by high-reaching glass, like a mannequin display at a storefront that no longer exists. Past them are several short tunnels with neon labels directing to each section held within the CICADA's wings.

"Welcome to CICADA. Next boarding takes place at 13:00. Do you have a ticket?"

I shake my head, palms clamming as she sweeps an arm across the glass dividing us. The sleek black uniform faded into a yellow gradient when it reaches each of their limbs, making them resemble a cicada in flight with a single wing in an unbalanced, tilted glide.

"Which cabin are you interested in boarding?"

The first time our parents bought us a flight ticket, you had asked if we could fly first class. We were stuck at the back of economy, but you didn't care because you had the window seat, and seeing the passing scenery, even if most of it was only clouds, was enough to bring you contentment. It was the physical journey you craved, the movement from one place to another. And though the flight from Toronto to Shanghai took almost fifteen hours, you marvelled at the tingle of your legs, the light-headedness of your drowsy mind, the ecstatic beating of your curious heart when you stepped off, hand in mine. *It feels like a transformation, like I'm a new person!* you said.

You said the same thing when we arrived on Station M. I felt no different, still feel no different. Travelling from one place to another, the simple journey, doesn't change who we are. However, staying in a place outside our home …

I skim the cabin options: *Reflection, Discussion, Escape, Happiness, Sadness, Anger,* among others.

At least, the cabins here aren't separated in the same vulgar and elitist ways where only the wealthy can buy comfortable journeys while the rest of us are crammed at the back of economy with little to no leg space and saltine crackers long past expiry. But one glimpse at the price shows me how our journeys are still overrun by capitalists, even when we are in a place of grief. When there is money to be made, there is no such thing as solace for our loss.

A passenger rushes out from the tunnel leading to the *Sadness* cabin, hands shielding their face, their body rattling more than it should, even given their zigzag fast walk. Another passenger pinches at the back of their neck, deep in thought, as they drag slow steps from *Discussion*, past me, skimming my shoulder as if I'm not there.

"Are you all right?"

Then my eyes land on *Mourning*.

"Yes."

I let go of the locket and point to the cabin option, my finger hovering in the middle of the attendant's face.

The stretch of a slow smile curves around each side of my finger, but what I see in their eyes, what their trained poised and unaffected expression attempts to hide, is pity. The same expression all those at the funeral had for you and me when our fathers passed. We didn't need it then, and I don't need it now.

They scan my face to initiate the payment. "Thank you for flying with the CICADA."

I nod my gratitude and head for *Mourning*.

On the glass panel screen the attendant gave me flickers an introductory brochure: a warning about exiting the CICADA from the back rather than where we enter; few passengers exit from the other end, most return to the lobby and leave where they started, because to exit from the end means they don't intend to return. At least, not to the same cabin; at least, not for a very long time. But I suppose this is how human nature is, we tend to move backwards, rewind all the progress we have already made, and start from the beginning—out of fear? Comfort?

Outside the tunnel leading to the *Mourning* cabin, floats exiled humans in pods, kept alive on IV nutrients until the Monitors deem them fit to return to society. Reintegration Simulations is what the news calls them. Really, they're just reinvented prisons. It's easier now for them to figure out whether someone is truly innocent or guilty, by digging into their memories, the same way they dug into yours. But by the time they discovered they falsely accused you, that the true culprit was hiding in the shadows of Station M after destroying their identity, it was already too late—you had already run out of breaths to take.

The culprit must be in one of the RS pods now. I hope they can never leave, but I also feel guilty for having the thought. Second chances were something you always believed in.

Stalled in front of the *Mourning* cabin, I wonder if I might feel the same as you did when you stepped off that plane, like a new person, even if I have yet to travel anywhere.

In *Mourning,* there are fewer people than expected, most passengers huddle in groups or pairs.

Most seats are closed off.

One person sits alone.

From behind, they resemble you, but when my steps pause next to them, the stranger's voice, the strained and suppressed tone, the slight dip in between their brows, lips parted, intaking slow but shallow breaths, reminds me of myself. Their legs are drawn up, face half hidden in between the knobby knees pressed against their chest. They are me—three months ago. They are me—now.

They look up, their short bob unruly, and offer a gaze of recognition even though we have never met before.

"I've been waiting for you," they say.

Rather than shock, I feel a strange sense of sadness. I look around. Maybe they are speaking to someone else, but within, I understand, they are speaking to me as I am speaking to them, in silence.

I settle myself into the seat next to them, the squeaking leather louder than my thoughts, and draw my knees up, cradling the limbs the same way as this stranger-friend.

"I'm here," I say.

"Yes."

We sit in silence. They don't need to speak for me to feel their loss, a hanging storm above their head, under their eyes, a shadow spreading from within their pupils and the cavern between their parted lips. I don't ask who they have lost, and they don't ask me.

"I'm here," they say, long after my eyes have glossed over, and my mind has drifted into the place between life and death.

"Yes."

Before I leave *Mourning,* I notice a few passengers wander through the door leading to the other end of the CICADA—a journey complete; a symbolic transformation, as the living insect had once represented—something that by itself cannot be extinct.

Back in the lobby, I feel as though I had gone to a faraway place, even though only an hour passed.

Tomorrow, I will again return to the CICADA, to *Mourning,* but it will not be for you; perhaps it'll be for the broken stranger-friend, but certainly, it will be for me. And I will continue to return, until the stranger-friend is no longer there, until I no longer want to rewind memories, until I have the courage to exit through the other end without turning back.

We Need to Talk....

Cora Buhlert

Okay, so I know this is awkward, but seriously, we need to talk.

I mean, I get it. Really, I do. I get that you guys are seriously lonely, considering that your species apparently doesn't have any females. And honestly, what the hell went wrong with evolution on your planet that your species has only males? I mean, how do you guys even reproduce?

Oh dear, I just realised.... You are male, aren't you? Because it's kind of hard to tell with you guys and if it turns out that you're not ... well, that would be really awkward, because I'm totally not a lesbian, if you know what I mean.

Anyway, assuming for now that you're male, I completely understand why you had to kidnap us. I mean, there's only dudes on your planet and all of you are kind of ... well, let's just say "not conventionally attractive"—so yeah, I get it. I understand why you felt the need to kidnap a bunch of random women from Earth, especially considering that fifty-one percent of us are female and many of us are pretty attractive.

And believe me, I feel flattered that I'm one of the chosen ones, one of those who were deemed attractive enough to be kidnapped. I mean, this is just like winning the intergalactic version of *America's Next Top Model*, only without Heidi Klum making nasty remarks about the size of your butt.

So in short, I'm flattered, I'm happy and I think this is totally awesome and cool.

But … and it really pains me to say this, believe me – this won't work. It just won't. Because at the end of the day, I'm still a human woman and you … well, I don't know the politically correct way to say this, but you are a bug-eyed monster.

In fact, you're the most bug-eyed bug-eyed monster I've ever seen. Those bug-eyed monsters on the covers of those old science-fiction magazines? They've got nothing on you, dude. Honestly, you're the king of the bug-eyed monsters, if I've ever seen one.

So really, it's not you, because you're awesome in all your bug-eyed glory. It's me.

I really don't want to hurt you, but honestly, pal, this won't work. It's not even that we don't speak the same language, because my friend Leticia ended up with a guy from Poland and she sure as hell didn't speak his language either. Nor is it that you're of a different race, cause I'm totally not racist and I think interracial relationships are totally cool, especially if the guy is really hot, if you know what I mean?

But we're just not compatible, okay? I mean, you don't even have the right equipment, so to say. Sure, you've got lots of appendices and tentacles and things like that, but you don't seem to have a penis, at least not as far as I can tell. Unless those tentacle-like things are penises, which would be both totally gross and totally awesome. And yes, I'm sure that tentacle sex is really hot, but … it's just not me, okay?

So in short, what I'm trying to say here is that you have to let me go. We can't have a proper physical or emotional relationship, because you don't talk and you can't have sex with me and I'm really not sure what you want of me, considering you just dragged me off to your alien cave to sit here, while you look at me. And by the way, dude, it's really bloody cold in here, so if you could turn up the heater, I'd be very, very obliged.

Okay, so maybe watching is how you dudes get it on. Hey, I'm not judging. I believe that everybody has the right to find satisfaction in their own way, as long as it's all between consenting adults.

But did you know that we have this absolutely marvellous invention called the Internet, which is full of that other marvellous invention called porn? So if you get it on by just watching, then the Internet has got you covered. It's got every type of porn imaginable and a couple of sorts you've never imagined. I mean, did I ever tell you about the time I came across that Furry porn site? And trust me, never ever google "bukkake."

So basically, what I'm trying to tell you here is that we can be friends, but we can never be more. I'm sorry, but that's just the way it is. We're simply too different on every level for this to ever work out.

So why don't you just return me and the other girls you guys kidnapped to Earth? I promise you there won't be any repercussions. We'll tell everybody that you were perfect gentlemen, because you were. I mean, you didn't even try to touch my breasts or my butt or any other interesting part of me, though you totally could have. And that fascination with my hands and feet—well, that's not a shocking fetish where I come from. Though if I'd known, I'd have brought my black stilettos and long opera gloves. Because you know, I can be a bit kinky, if I feel like it.

Still, why don't you just return me and the other girls you kidnapped home? I mean, you're clearly intelligent beings, seeing that you've got spaceships and high-tech caves and all. So I'm sure you'll see that this will never work out.

And if you take us home, we'd be eternally grateful. We could even give you dating tips and play wingwomen for you on your dates with bug-eyed girl monsters who are actually compatible with you.

I mean, there have to be female bug-eyed monster somewhere in this galaxy. Because anything else would be colossally unfair towards you guys and we really can't have that, because in the end you were pretty nice. The nicest bug-eyed monster that ever kidnapped me. Not that I really have anything to compare you to, since you're also the only bug-eyed monster that ever kidnapped me.

And yes, I know that it hurts to be rejected. But trust me when I tell you that everything will work out just fine in the end. I'll find a nice human boy and you'll find a nice bug-eyed girl monster and we'll all live happily ever after.

Disintegration

Michael Butterworth

"We first met one another at university. She was reading psychology, and I was taking a printing diploma at a nearby art college. We both had similar interests, and opposite characters.

"I think that I was the more stable of the two. She was frightened of life, and unsure of herself. Her interest in psychology was most probably in part a symptom of her state of mind, for I rarely got the impression that she was studying for the sake of her career. It was a strange choice for her, and it didn't really lead her anywhere except, as I now see, deeper into her own mind."

Because of her fear of people, she had no faith in human nature. In the case of ninety-nine per cent of people she met, I would say that she had good cause to suspect their motives towards her. But she could not bring herself to trust even the one per cent who are always trustworthy and warm of affection. I fell in love with her, but it took me six years of married life to convince her of that fact.

"We married suddenly, two months after we met. I gave up my printing course; she decided to stay on at university. I was a bit irritated at this, though I hid my feelings and encouraged her, in the hope that she would one day come out of her shell and think of her career and her future rather than use, as she did, her psychology course as a tool with which to dwell upon the past."

> And what a past! She was the product of a dissatisfied marriage, of parents who argued continually, and who looked upon their children as a source of their unhappiness. As she was the most sensitive of the three, she was also the one who grew up most affected by the obvious rift in her parents' relationship and the physical beating-ups of her and her mother by her father.

"We had a succession of flats, and eventually a house and children of our own. Her course at the university was completed, though as I suspected she would she failed the final examination. As, by this time, I had won her over she was not too upset. She did not attempt to resit the exam but resigned herself instead to family life with me.

"All went well for several years until one morning we had a cable sent to us from an old friend, who in the interim had become head of a psychology research centre. Neither she nor I had severed relationships with our old friends and kept ourselves thoroughly up to date about their work. A mound of literature came through our door each week, the outcome of subscriptions to just about every relevant journal on mental research."

> I suppose that having exhausted its search for knowledge on the purely physical plain, and succeeded in conquering its birth planet and, also interstellar space, the human race felt that it was now beneficial to its survival to turn its attention inwards, at its origin. There were still many social and living problems that had to be solved amongst the inhabitants of earth. Research of this kind,

scientific investigation of the previously scorned powers of the human mind such as telepathy, telekinesis, the power to create, and so on, had become popular.

"Thom's cable could not have come at a better time for both of us. We were at the peak of a scientific hubbub. It stated briefly, without mincing words, that he needed 'guinea pigs' to take part in a consciousness-swapping experiment. He remembered that she was a particularly susceptible person, with an easily opened mind, ideally suited. Because he could think of 'absolutely no one else' he had been forced to turn to us, despite our family ties. We both agreed to help him, a rather foolish decision I now admit."

At the time, however, we were blinded by an altruistic feeling of desire to martyr ourselves for the sake of scientific advancement.

"We had some guilty feelings about leaving our children but, we reasoned, the research would not take more than a few weeks at most and we would soon return.

"We left our children in care of an aunt, paid off a few months' mortgage repayments on the house, and left at once, all expenses paid by courtesy of the Lockwood Psychology Research Foundation.

"Thom—Dr. Thomas Brown—is a fat, perspiring man, very patient and dedicated. As is the case with many research scientists that I have met he has cultivated a kind of dual character. On the one hand he is humane and considerate, on the other he is a ruthless exploiter; an ideal formula for a man who has both family and self-survival interests at heart. But in Thom, the instinct to survive ..."

... sublimated nowadays as the exploration of inner space rather than geographical investigation of the unknown...

"… has gained the upper hand. Although he likes to be responsible, his thirst for knowledge causes him to have a unique morality unparalleled in any other person I have known, except perhaps in the monstrous scientists of the old horror movies who used fellow humans in the performance of some cruel experiment or other."

Odd as it may seem, despite his great intelligence, I don't think he is consciously aware of this. As is the case with many such professional men, the subject's compliance is regarded as pure good-naturedness. It does not occur to him that she is unaware of danger, that her enthusiasm may be the enthusiasm of the naive: well-intentioned but foolhardy. It was with this sort of benevolent blinkeredness I am sure, that Thom accepted our decision to help.

"He received us well, and entertained us with dinners, drinks and stories. For much of the time, as it would be with three enthusiasts keen to explore the human mind, our conversation was about psychology, the people in the field and the discoveries being made. It was pretty evident that he thought his Foundation was on to a shattering breakthrough. The idea, he eventually confided in us, had enraptured him throughout his adult life: a world in which mental communication could become an everyday reality. It was not only his vision. Communication of the sort he envisaged has always been a preoccupation. But Thom had been especially haunted by the idea, and the situation as we found it at his Foundation was, that, after years of study as a student and after further years of post-graduate research and then as a professor his team had designed an apparatus he was confident could freely transmit thought from one human being to another."

As yet, a thought could be transmitted no great distance, only the length of a piece of cable: in order to receive and transmit at all, the brains of two participants had to be attached by cable to the apparatus, one transmitting his thoughts into the apparatus, and the other receiving the same thoughts from it. In effect the apparatus was a media device, and although a block in the development of instantaneous communication (telepathy), nevertheless it was a first step in that direction. It was the first stage, and Thom was both proud and excited.

"We were shown the apparatus and a date was fixed for the experiment. Because of the numerous experimental conditions that had to be right before the main experiment could take place, we were, in the meantime, kept busy performing tests, both on ourselves and on the apparatus. One of the tests, I remember, was arranged to determine the speed of flow of our thoughts, another determined the clarity of our thinking. To test the equipment, a one word thought of mine was successfully transmitted to Helen, and vice versa."

Thom had told us that actual thought transference, once considered a remarkable achievement, was accomplished daily by his laboratory staff, and was only used now as a test. What Thom was after was the transference of one entire mind into the mind of another, in the hope of setting off a correspondence between the two. He was working on the assumption that the computation of one single thought could be the mathematical basis for the transference of an entire matrix. The computation would be long and complicated, but he was confident of success.

"The day arrived at last. We had been waiting in nervous anticipation of this moment. Helen was wired up first, then I. There were no electrodes, only a sheet of what Thom called 'thought-sensitive' material, which was fitted to the inside of a rubber 'cap'. This headpiece was tailored to cover the whole head, neck, chest and back. The only inlet was an air pipe, which fed our noses."

From her headpiece a maze of coloured wires led into a row of input sockets on the instrument (I say "instrument"—in fact the apparatus was composed of many instruments so voluminous that they filled our sizeable laboratory), for the idea at first was to transfer her mind into mine. My headpiece was thus attached by wires to a row of output sockets. After a while, Thom told us, it would be possible, by throwing a switch, to reverse the flow: my mind in her body, her mind in my body. The third stage of the experiment (and the highlight) would be the evacuation of both our minds from our bodies. Our separate minds would be stored in separate banks of the computer, and he hoped we would be allowed to communicate at a speed approaching that of thought. Finally, our minds would be returned to our bodies, the computer's memory having recorded every detail of the encounter of our minds.

Some hours were spent by technicians fiddling with bits of the apparatus, to stabilise conditions. Then Thom gave the order to commence. Juice was turned on,
  and I began to feel the familiar tingling in
  my brain cells that had characterised earlier
experiments when we had been engaged in
  the transference of single thoughts. Then,
without warning, my senses were cut off – an
entirely new experience. I could not see, hear, feel,

taste, or touch. My first reaction was to panic, but
as the state was not altogether uncomfortable (in fact
it was quite pleasant), I soon calmed down. It was a
bit like being in a sleep state where, identically, the
five senses are curtailed. But, by contrast, I retained
awareness: not the familiar awareness of my five known
senses but presumably that of my mystical 'sixth' sense.
My 'psychic' state also differed from my normal sleep state
in that I experienced no dreaming, though I felt that, had the
dream imagery come to me I could easily have controlled it.
This was a pleasant feeling, for I have long desired to be able
to control my dreams. There were no images—only void. I
could not sense the particles which made up my new body.
I knew I was, and that I was 'there', and that was all. The
condition did not alarm me, nor was it boring. I felt contented.
After a while I became conscious of an approaching
"something', which I assumed must be Helen. A moment
later, her consciousness had merged with mine. Hers was quite
different to my own, and its approach had filled me with anxiety.
I realised why as soon as we became one mind: she was frightened
and could not succumb to the relaxation that had overcome
me. She was full of spikes, and filled me with gaps. No words
were exchanged, only feelings. By conveying to her a feeling
of protection, I was able to calm her somewhat. A great part of
her fright was dispelled at having found something to hide in.
She had hardly had time to pulse more than a wave or so of her
sweet feelings of gratitude into me, when I felt myself suddenly
grow distant from her. I found myself in an area much the same
as the first had been, before she had joined me, and assumed that
Thom had now transferred my mind into her unoccupied brain.
I felt pleasure, for the experiment was progressing well, and
the second stage was almost over. But I was concerned for my
partner and hoped that by now she had overcome her fears. But
she had not, and I think that it was possibly her resistance to the
whole affair that brought about her fate. Thom, absorbed by the

manipulation of our minds, had neglected to provide us with any means of communication with the world he inhabited. She could not protest. She had been moved pawn-like to an area identical with mine but separate from it. I was made aware of this fact by her extremely clear thoughts that pierced through the void like needles. On this occasion, no doubt because of our detachment from one another, our thoughts were transmitted in the form of words and pictures, as well as feelings. She was still in a state of panic, but having realised that I was close by, and that so far there had been no catastrophe, she communicated with greater objectivity. She told me that it had been silly of her to behave the way she had, and of how lost she had felt when Thom had suddenly taken me from her. What she said sounded ridiculous. I laughed, for the picture that her words invoked in me was one of Thom and I having an affair. Part of me knew that this interpretation was not what she had meant, and perfectly understood her real meaning, but it seemed to me that this sort of punning and literal acceptance of words was acceptable to both of us, even desirable. I wanted to break down the conditioning power of words, which I saw as invented tools that only partially did their designed job of controlling communicated true feeling. She must have agreed with me, for a moment later she "laughed." After we had made a pact not to use words except for the conveyance of specific information, we each settled down to our own 'place', meaning to become more intimately attached. (The area between us was a sharp barrier, separating us by what seemed infinity, which was in fact only a few computer banks. Living in this mental limbo, was an existence uncomplicated by quantified physical measurements of space, matter, and time, for the three elements did not exist in quite the same way as they appear to exist to us out here in the five-sense world.) There was not much time to spend together before I was suddenly made conscious of the fact that communication from her had ceased. That moment was the worst I have experienced in my life. There was a sort of 'explosion' of images from her, in which her mind was completely opened and laid bare. Her entire life's experiences came out, a human wreckage that floated in pieces through my existence. Instantly I knew everything about her, who she was, and why she was. My understanding of her as a person gained over long years of marriage was nothing compared with the intensity with which I knew her in that single instant. The frail, unworkable structure she had given her mind, with the desperate intention to stave off the cruelties of life, had collapsed. The grim determination she had used to hold it all together, was dissipated. Then, as quickly, every trace of her mind had gone, melted like overnight snow. There was no question of her merely having stopped communicating. She had gone. Simultaneously, I received a terrible pain that burst explosively from my centre and that spread outwards towards my extremities. I endured this for a split second. Then I "awoke."

Images of the laboratory were swimming before my eyes, jumbled and incoherent. My hand was pressed against my head, to ease the pain, which had somehow concentrated there. Thom's face came into my field of vision, someone pulled down my arms, and my headpiece was removed. I lost consciousness and awoke in bed in the Foundation sick room.

"Later, Thom came in to inform me that she was dead. That's really where the story ends, except to say that the news that Thom brought to me was already old in my head. I had experienced her death alongside her.

"After planning for her disintegration, I left with a bad headache and one or two other ailments that come and go, symptoms that

Thom assures me will clear up gradually over a period of years. Not much comfort."

"And she was right," my listener interrupted. "Thom had taken you away from her."

"Yes. Only not in the manner we had thought, ironically. There's been no affair!" I managed a sardonic laugh. "I view it all as a scientific experiment—perhaps a very good one—that went wrong. Thom was as white as death, the most upset man I have seen. He was ninety percent directly responsible for her death."

My listener drew me to her. I let her cradle me, but I could feel no emotion of the kind she might have expected me to have. My mind was still too much preoccupied with thoughts of unfaithfulness. I lay stiffly against her breast. Whether she realised my dilemma or not, I could not say, but a moment later she let me go. I arose and rescued my drink from the bar top where I had left it half an hour ago.

Publication History

"Cortellian Rain" by Jonathan Nevair first appeared in *Simultaneous Times* Episode 46, December 2021.

"Sibling Rivalry" by F. J. Bergmann first appeared in *Simultaneous Times* Episode 48, February 2022.

"trAIn" by Brent A. Harris first appeared in *Simultaneous Times* Episode 17, July 2019.

"Manhunt" by Gideon Marcus first appeared in *Simultaneous Times* Episode 36, February 2021.

"Juliet & Juliet(te): A Romance of Alternate Worlds" by A. C. Wise

First appeared in *The Kissing Booth Girl and Other Stories* by A. C. Wise (Lethe Press, 2016).

"In the City of Wrestling Kudzu" by Tara Campbell appears for the first time in this collection.

"An Ever-Reddening Glow" by David Brin first appeared in *Analog,* February 1996, ed. Stanley Schmidt.

"At My Fingertips" by Robin Rose Graves first appeared in *Simultaneous Times* Episode 34, December 2020.

"Faster Than Light Can Carry You" by Renan Bernardo appears for the first time in this collection.

"The Duelist" by Christopher Ruocchio first appeared in *Simultaneous Times* Episode 22, December 2019.

"Hidden Underneath" by Toshiya Kamei first appeared in *Simultaneous Times* Episode 39, May 2021.

"Reaction Shot" by Todd Sullivan first appeared in *Simultaneous Times* Episode 54, August 2022.

"The Two-Faced Miracle of Justice Father Win" by Susan Rukeyser first appeared in *Simultaneous Times* Episode 54, August 2022.

"A Journey Without Movement" by Ai Jiang appears for the first time in this collection.

"We Need to Talk...." by Cora Buhlert first appeared in *Bug Eyed Monsters and the Women Who Love Them* by Cora Buhlert (Pegasus Pulp Publishing, 2015).

"Disintegration" by Michael Butterworth first appeared in *New Worlds Quarterly* #6, 1973, eds. Michael Moorcock & Charles Platt.

Contributor Biographies

Jonathan Nevair is a speculative fiction author and, as Dr. Jonathan Wallis, an art historian and Professor of Art History at Moore College of Art & Design, Philadelphia. After two decades of academic teaching and publishing, he finally got up the nerve to write fiction. **jonathannevair.com**

When galactic danger calls, Agent Renault answers.

Strange signals pulse from an icy planet in a remote star system. Enter Lilline Renault, GAM-OPs secret agent extraordinaire. To ordinary citizens she's Keely Larkin, an adventure company guide with a flair for the daring and a penchant for writing trite poetry.

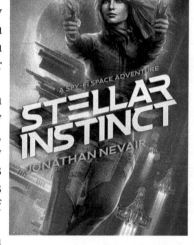

When the mission takes an unexpected turn into virtual reality gaming and terrifying cosmic forces, Lilline leaps into action. Verses flow as she rockets through space, dons cunning disguises, and infiltrates enemy territory with an arsenal of secret gadgets.

To solve the mystery behind a dastardly plan means beating a mastermind at his own game. Lilline will need her best weapon to stand a fighting chance: her instinct.

STELLAR INSTINCT: a standalone interstellar espionage thriller

---

F. J. Bergmann is the poetry editor of *Mobius: The Journal of Social Change* (**mobiusmagazine.com**) and freelances as a copy editor and book designer. She lives in Wisconsin and fantasizes about tragedies on or near exoplanets. She was a Writers of the Future winner. Her work has

appeared in *Abyss & Apex, Analog, Asimov's SF,* and elsewhere in the alphabet. She has competed at National Poetry Slam with the Madison Urban Spoken Word slam team. While lacking academic literary qualifications, she is kind to those so encumbered. She used to work with horses. She thinks imagination can compensate for anything. **fjbergmann.com**

Consider the feelings of books you read.
It's said that pages whisper as they ruffle, but sometimes even ordinary books talk to themselves or chat with other books in a bookcase or library—a community of bookish entities—each with its own literary or not-so-literary agenda.

SHELF LIFE: the secret thoughts of books
Forthcoming in 2023 from Space Cowboy Books

BRENT A. HARRIS is a two-time Sidewise Award finalist of alternate history who writes about dinosaurs, fantasy, the fears of our future and the mistakes of our past. When not writing speculative fiction, he focuses on his family, playing board games with friends, and talking nerdy. He holds a Masters degree in Creative Writing from National University as an NU Scholar. While he considers California his home, he currently resides abroad in Okinawa, Japan. **brentaharris.com**

Twilight of the Mesozoic Moon and Other Time Travel Twists
Dinosaurs. Time-traveling astronaut dinosaurs. Really, that's all this blurb had to say, right? What else could you want? I know I'd buy it. I mean, that's literally why I wrote it, because who doesn't want stories about time-traveling astronaut dinosaurs?

But if you're hard to please, there's a smattering of other sci-fi stories in this collection by two-time Sidewise Award nominated author Brent A Harris (that's me!). Most of these stories have been printed in the award-winning Tales from Alternate Earths series, other anthologies, and podcasts. But not all of you have read them (or read them all). So, this is a great place to start.

And! There are a couple of exclusive stories within, including a dinosaur displaced into Victorian times creating dinosaur-sized problems for his rescuers. If dinosaurs aren't to your liking then there's time-traveling stories inspired by *Star Trek* and *Quantum Leap* that you can ponder over instead all comfy cozy on your couch or oversized chair with your cup of Earl Grey. Hot.

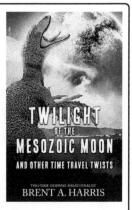

Award-winning science fiction author **GIDEON MARCUS** has just finished *Hyvilma*, third book in The Kitra Saga, a YA space adventure series featuring themes of isolation, teamwork, and hope, and starring a queer protagonist of color. His short fiction can be found in *Dark Matter, Utopia*, and elsewhere. He is also the editor of the Rediscovery: Science Fiction by Women anthology series, featuring some of the best works of SF's Silver Age, and the founder of Journey Press, an independent publisher focused on unusual and diverse speculative fiction. A four-time Hugo Finalist, he runs the time machine project Galactic Journey. He is a professional space historian, member of the American Astronautical Society's history committee, and a much-sought-after public speaker. Gideon lives in San Diego County with his writer/editor wife and their Hugo-nominated artist daughter … along with a cat, a snake, and an immense library. **gideonmarcus.com**

The **Lodestar***-longlisted Kitra saga continues!*
Follow the space adventure exploits of Captain Kitra Yilmaz and her diverse found family of crew as they find themselves in increasing peril and fame at the edge of the interstellar Frontier. A YA series for all ages featuring thrills, romance, good science, and Pinky's puns. With illustrations by Hugo Finalist Lorelei Esther!

A. C. WISE is the author of the novels *Wendy, Darling* and *Hooked,* along with the recent short story collection *The Ghost Sequences.* Her work has won the Sunburst Award and been a finalist for the Nebula, Stoker, World Fantasy, British Fantasy, Locus, Aurora, Lambda, Jackson, and Ignyte Awards. In addition to her fiction, she contributes a review column to *Apex Magazine.* Find her online at **acwise.net**.

Wendy, Darling

When Peter Pan reappears in Wendy Darling's life years after her childhood adventures in Neverland and kidnaps her daughter, Wendy sets off in pursuit of her former friend, vowing to stop at nothing to bring her daughter home.

A dark, feminist re-imagining of the story of Neverland and Peter Pan.

TARA CAMPBELL is an award-winning writer, teacher, Kimbilio Fellow, fiction co-editor at *Barrelhouse,* and graduate of American University's MFA in Creative Writing. She teaches creative writing at venues such as American University, Johns Hopkins University, Clarion West, The Writer's Center, Hugo House, and the National Gallery of Art. Publication credits include *Masters Review, Wigleaf, Electric Literature, CRAFT Literary,*

Daily Science Fiction, Strange Horizons, and *Escape Pod/Artemis Rising.* She's the author of a novel, two hybrid collections of poetry and prose, and two short story collections from feminist sci-fi publisher Aqueduct Press. Find her at **taracampbell.com**.

Cabinet of Wrath: A Doll Collection

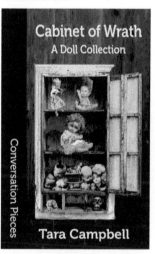

Deep in the recesses of childhood memory, your old playthings await. Come take a peek inside the Cabinet of Wrath to find out what really happens when toys go missing, and the stark decision they must make if they ever want to go home again. Discover what doll heads really think about being separated from their bodies. Follow a skull-and-bones novelty ring as it assembles a full body for itself, bit by grisly bit, and learn how loving your doll too much can lead to grave consequences. Visit **cabinetofwrath.com** and open the door to a playtime you'll never forget.

DAVID BRIN is a scientist, tech speaker/consultant, and author. His novels about our survival and opportunities in the near future are *Earth* and *Existence.* A film by Kevin Costner was based on *The Postman.* His 16 novels, including NY Times Bestsellers and Hugo Award winners, have been translated into more than twenty languages. *Earth* foreshadowed global warming, cyberwarfare and the world wide web. An advisor to NASA's Innovative & Advanced Concepts program, David appears frequently on shows such as *Nova* and *The Universe* and *Life After People,* speaking about science and future trends. His first nonfiction book—*The Transparent Society: Will Technology Make Us Choose Between Freedom and Privacy?*—won the Freedom of Speech Award of the American Library Association. His second nonfiction book is *Vivid Tomorrows: Science Fiction and Hollywood* (2021). **davidbrin.com**

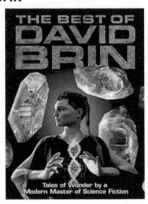

The Best of David Brin

David Brin has thrilled readers in almost thirty languages by presenting vastly imaginative—and well-grounded—challenges set in times that might yet come … along with a sometimes razor-thin hope we'll persevere. In this major retrospective collection of shorter work, gathered from across an extraordinary career spanning decades, you'll find wonder via David Brin's unparalleled talent at imagination, extrapolation, hard-headed optimism, and plain old fun.

ROBIN ROSE GRAVES is a science fiction writer and poet. Previous works of hers have appeared in *Dark Matter, The Starlight SciFaiku Review, Star*Line,* and *Simultaneous Times Podcast.* She is an editor at Android Press and a frequent contributor to the *Galactic Journey.* She runs the science fiction BookTube channel, *The Book Wormhole.* **youtube.com/@ TheBookWormhole**

Science Fiction from the
PAST
PRESENT
&
FUTURE
by Robin Rose Graves

For *Science Fiction from the Past Present and Future*, go to the *Book Wormhole*, only on Youtube.

RENAN BERNARDO is a science fiction and fantasy writer from Rio de Janeiro, Brazil. His fiction appears in *Apex Magazine, Podcastle, Escape Pod, Daily Science Fiction, Future Science Fiction, Solarpunk Magazine,* and others. His Solarpunk/Clifi short fiction collection, *Different Kinds of Defiance,* is forthcoming from Android Press. His fiction has appeared in multiple languages including German, Italian, Japanese, and Portuguese. Find him on Twitter (@RenanBernardo) and at **renanbernardo.com**.

CHRISTOPHER RUOCCHIO is the internationally award-winning author of the Sun Eater series, blending elements of science fiction and fantasy, as well as more than twenty works of short fiction. Born and raised in Raleigh, NC, Christopher received a degree in English Rhetoric from North Carolina State University in 2015, with a minor in the Classics, when he began a career in publishing, serving as the Junior Editor at Baen Books until the summer of 2021, when he resigned to take up the life of a full-time writer. Christopher sold his first novel, *Empire of Silence,* at 22. *Empire of Silence* won the Manly Wade Wellman Award for Best Novel in 2019, as well as the Hellfest Literary Prize in 2021. His subsequent novels were twice nominated for the Dragon Award. His books have appeared in 5 languages. He curated 8 short story anthologies for Baen Books, including *Sword & Planet, Time Troopers,* and *Worlds Long Lost.* His work has also appeared in Marvel Comics. Christopher lives in Raleigh, North Carolina with his family. **sollanempire.com**

Epic fantasy? Space opera? Is it too much to ask for both?
It was not his war.

The galaxy remembers him as a hero: the man who burned every last alien Cielcin from the sky. They remember him as a monster: the devil who destroyed a sun, casually annihilating four billion human lives—even the Emperor himself—against Imperial orders.

But Hadrian was not a hero. He was not a monster. He was not even a soldier.

On the wrong planet, at the right time, for the best reasons, Hadrian Marlowe starts down a path that can only end in fire. He flees his father and a future as a torturer only to be left stranded on a strange, backwater world.

Forced to fight as a gladiator and navigate the intrigues of a foreign planetary court, Hadrian must fight a war he did not start, for an Empire he does not love, against an enemy he will never understand.

THE SUN EATER SERIES *by*
Christopher Ruocchio

TOSHIYA KAMEI is an Asian writer who takes inspiration from fairy tales, folklore, and mythology. Their short stories have appeared in *Daily Science Fiction, Galaxy's Edge,* and elsewhere. Their piece "Hungry Moon" won *Apex Magazine*'s October 2022 Microfiction Contest.

TODD SULLIVAN currently lives in Seoul, South Korea, where he teaches English as a Second Language. He has had more than two dozen short stories, poems, essays, and novelettes published across five countries. He currently has two book series through indie publishers in America. He writes for a Taipei web and play series that focuses upon black and African narratives. He founded the online magazine *Samjoko* in 2021 and hosts a YouTube Channel that interviews writers across the publishing spectrum.
samjokomagazine.com

In a world of swords and sorcery, illusionist Kim Nam-Gi has a dream: to become a hero.

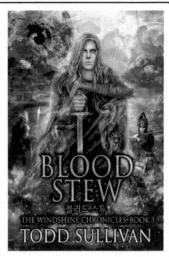

Born in the land of South Hanguk, cursed with a malformed spine, Nam-Gi longs to prove his worth against dragons and monsters. Instead, he toils in his family's restaurant while studying advanced spells under the tutelage of a Dark Elf.

When his father, Kim Joo-Won, goes deep into debt in an attempt to attract new customers to their struggling restaurant, Nam-Gi is once again denied permission to put his name forward on the governor's registry. Joo-Won needs him for the restaurant, and a greedy money lender hovers over them with the aim to keep the Kim family in perpetual debt.

Desperate to solve their financial woes, Nam-Gi uses magic to trick customers into believing that the restaurant's meager offerings are actually carp and abalone. If he can keep up the deception, his family might prosper enough to escape the lender. Then his father may grant him permission to abandon his post and take the challenge of a quest.

A perfect opportunity soon arrives. Two fishermen discover a corpse with strange leathery wings drifting in the sea. They haul the body back to the village. Tragedy ensues when their unexpected catch proves to be more terrifying than anything they could have imagined.

The governors of South Hanguk seek out adventurers who can slay the monster that now terrorizes the besieged fisherfolk. Will Nam-Gi be allowed to roam across wild lands and wander through dark forests to vanquish this threat? Can he push his crippled body beyond the limits that have plagued him since birth?

Find out in **BLOOD STEW**, the tale of a disabled teen who must face overwhelming odds in his quest to become a hero.

SUSAN RUKEYSER co-created Joshua Tree's Desert Split Open, which hosts literary events for work that is feminist, queer, or otherwise radical. Her debut novel, *Not On Fire, Only Dying*, was published by Twisted Road Publications, and her new novel, *The Worst Kind of Girl*,

is forthcoming from Braddock Avenue Books. Susan's feminist science fiction appears in Vol. 2 of the *Simultaneous Times Anthology*, and on episodes 18, 29, and 54 of the *Simultaneous Times* podcast. **susanrukeyser.com**

Feminist, of course. It gets a little political.

Strange signals pulse from an icy planet in a remote star system. Enter **UTILITY LOCATION**, a multimedia micro-memoir, pairing tiny prose-poems with cellphone snapshots of spraypainted street markings. It's a book about being jumbled, out of place, in search of signs. It's about the pull toward darkness and also light, and the many people we become, across a lifetime. The result is a tough, shorthand, diaristic, imprecise, and contemplative review of a life so far. (24 pp, Bottlecap Press, 2022) **bottlecap.press/products/utility**

AI JIANG is a Chinese-Canadian writer, a Nebula Award finalist, and an immigrant from Fujian. She is a member of HWA, SFWA, and Codex. Her work can be found in *F&SF, The Dark, Uncanny*, among others. She is the recipient of Odyssey Workshop's 2022 Fresh Voices Scholarship and the author of *Linghun* and *I AM AI*. Find her on Twitter @AiJiang_ and online at **aijiang.ca**.

I AM AI

If you had the opportunity to give up humanity for efficiency, mechanical invincibility, and to surpass human limitations ... would you?

Ai is a cyborg, under the guise of an AI writing program, who struggles to keep up with the never-blinking city of Emit as it threatens to leave all those like her behind.

CORA BUHLERT was born and bred in Bremen, North Germany, where she still lives today—after time spent in London, Singapore, Rotterdam and Mississippi. Cora holds an MA degree in English from the University of Bremen. Cora has been writing since she was a teenager and has published stories, articles and poetry in various international magazines. Cora is the winner of the 2022 Hugo Award for Best Fan Writer and the 2021 Space Cowboy Award. When she is not writing, she works as a translator and teacher. Visit her on the web at **corabuhlert.com** or follow her on Twitter @CoraBuhlert.

Bug-Eyes Monsters and the Women Who Love Them

Six short science fiction stories that subvert the tropes and clichés of the golden age and caricature the gender dynamics of classic science fiction.

You'll travel from suburban America to the farthest reaches of the galaxy. You'll visit New Pluto City and Garrett's World. You'll encounter the terrors of the Brazilian jungle and the horrors of American suburbia. You'll meet phantom lovers and alien she-devils, devious man-eaters, unseen underwater monsters and the tentacled menace of the fearsome Eee'chuk-chi'up, dashing space heroes who don't get the girl and bug-eyed monsters that do. And you'll meet intergalactic heroines who know exactly what they want from a lover.

MICHAEL BUTTERWORTH is a UK author, publisher and editor. He was a key part of the UK New Wave of Science Fiction in the 1960s, contributing fiction to *New Worlds* and other publications. In 1975 he founded Savoy

Books with David Britton, co-authoring Britton's controversial novel *Lord Horror,* an absurdist treatment of demagoguery and anti-Semitism as espoused by "Hitler's Englishman" William Joyce (aka Lord Haw-Haw). In 2009 Butterworth launched the contemporary visual art and writing journal, *Corridor8.* His latest works are *Complete Poems: 1965–2020* (Space Cowboy Books 2023), selected readings from this (also Space Cowboy Books 2023) set to music and available on CD and bandcamp, the eponymously titled *Butterworth* (NULL23, 2019) that collects his fiction from *New Worlds* and *Emanations,* and *My Servant the Wind,* a novel (also NULL23, 2019). Author photo by Danny Moran. **michael-butterworth.co.uk**

Complete Poems: 1965–2020 brings to more deserving attention a less heard voice in modern poetry.

For more than fifty years Michael Butterworth, better known for his work as a writer, editor and publisher, has also been a quiet, unobtrusive voice in poetry, with roots lying both in the small press poetry journals of the sixties and seventies and in the New Wave of Science Fiction. His work is distinguished as much for the restless intelligence, wit and intimacy of his voice as a determination, shown in many of these poems, to paint metaphorical pictures of the perils we face due to our poor regard for the fragile biosphere in

which we live. In other poems, he finds, within the events of an ordinary life, scope for the transcendent, and in still others his use of nonsense and absurdity playfully captures the moment, puncturing the illusions of the self. Across his work, elements are reiterated but endlessly transfigured....

The effect is at once familiar and yet profound, in language that has the confessional qualities and simplicity of early influences such as Sylvia Plath and the Beats, and the later influence of Zen poets such as

Ryōkan. Occasionally the writing is startlingly radical—a reminder of the poet's beginnings in the New Wave.

A collection such as this one from Space Cowboy Books is overdue, and ***Complete Poems: 1965–2020*** brings to more deserving attention a less heard voice in modern poetry.

AUSTIN HART is a painter and graphic designer from Southern California. He lives in Morongo Valley with his wife, cat and two goats. **austinh.art**

Milton Keynes UK
Ingram Content Group UK Ltd.
UKHW010800080923
428296UK00001B/137